A MAN WORTH LOVING

Karen Rose Smith

A KISMET™ Romance

METEOR PUBLISHING CORPORATION
Bensalem, Pennsylvania

To my husband, Steve,
for believing in the dream with me.

KAREN ROSE SMITH

Karen Rose Smith is a former English teacher. When back surgery interrupted her lifestyle, writing romances became a creative and emotional outlet. Karen resides in Pennsylvania with her husband of twenty years and their nineteen-year-old son. Besides reading and writing, she dabbles in watercolor and oil painting.

PROLOGUE

Every fifteen minutes fire sirens screamed. Flames raced up the brick warehouse and licked fiercely at the roof. Streams of water from fire hoses ineffectually shot at the blaze eating the building that occupied half a city block.

Nate McKendrick zipped his down jacket as he stepped inside the cordoned-off area and spoke to a policeman. Edging as close as he could to the flaming building, he aimed his camera at the hookies ventilating the fire, making a place for it to escape. His reporter was covering the scene from the other end of the block, but Nate wanted to get these pictures himself. The old thirst for adventure couldn't be quenched. Just like water couldn't quench the flames.

Suddenly, above the fracas, Nate heard a fireman yell, "Somebody help! It's Jim Nolan. He went in too far without his mask. The walls are collapsing and he's trapped inside!"

Nate dropped the camera until it ʼwung on his neck.

7

His long legs eliminated the distance between him and the commotion as he swore. Nolan. Of all people. He and Shara were getting a divorce. Did that have anything to do with his recklessness?

Nate stopped statue-still as he saw a fireman run toward him with a limp body swung over his shoulders. Watching the paramedics work frantically over the still form, Nate knew the verdict before they could confirm it. Jim Nolan had risked his neck one too many times. Nate felt numb. The hell of it was he understood the fireman's addiction— the thrill of fighting a blaze or, in his own case, capturing on film a power bigger than man. He raked his fingers through hair as black as the smoke rising in front of him. Thank God, he had never been careless.

Shara had to be told. Better it came from him than a stranger. He decided not to think further than that.

As Shara took the carton of milk from the refrigerator and poured herself a glass, she thought of the life she was carrying inside her. Should she tell Jim now, or wait until the divorce was final? What if she told him and he contested the divorce? What if he used the baby as a weapon to keep her tied to him? He wanted to stay married, but he didn't want a marriage.

Her feelings didn't count. Her fears didn't count. He spent more time at the fire station than at home. Double the time? Triple the time? Fighting fires and hanging out with the guys held more allure than *she* ever could. A child wouldn't make a difference. He'd be just as irresponsible, just as insensitive as he was now.

Shara thought about why she'd married him. He was boyish, exciting, and she'd badly needed someone to love. But after six months, she'd known the marriage was a miserable mistake. They should have divorced before now. Somehow, he'd always talked her out of it. He'd played on her guilt, her need not to fail.

He'd tried to talk her out of it the night this baby was conceived. He'd been charming, conciliatory. Because she'd been nervous, she'd drunk too much of the wine he'd brought and insisted she drink. He'd taken advantage of that and her sense of failure for the unworkable marriage. When he'd left that night, she'd been more certain than ever a divorce was the only road to take.

Before they'd married, Jim said he wanted children. It wasn't until the ring was on her finger that she realized he wanted to have the fun of fathering without the responsibility of caring. He wasn't so different from her stepfather. Only her stepfather had paid someone to take care of her rather than dumping the burden on his wife. Was there a man alive who could be an attentive husband and a loving father? Her experience told her no.

Rubbing her stomach lightly, Shara smiled. She'd love this child more than any child *could* be loved. The happiness she felt outweighed any worries she entertained about the divorce. She drank the glass of milk slowly, knowing it would nourish her baby.

She was rinsing the glass in the sink when the doorbell rang. When she opened the door, she saw Nate McKendrick, a friend, the owner of *The Herald*. His face was streaked with soot, his camera hung crookedly at his chest.

He stood immobile for a moment, towering a good four inches above her. "Can I come in?"

She squeezed the question through her throat. "What's happened, Nate?"

He stepped inside, bringing with him the stench of smoke. "I was at the fire getting some pictures when I heard a fireman shout. Jim went in too far without his mask. The walls collapsed and he was trapped. He took one too many chances. Shara, I don't know how to say this . . . He's dead.''

"Oh, my God! He said he had nine lives. He said—"

"Jim's dead," Nate repeated softly but firmly, as if trying to make her realize the fact.

Shara's denial coincided with another wail of the siren. When she looked as if she might pass out, Nate swung his camera to the side and closed her in his arms, clutching her tight against his chest. Burying his chin in her long brown hair, he knew it didn't matter who was holding her, she just needed to be held until she absorbed the shock. With her in his arms, his body trembled, and he swore because he had no right to feel what he was feeling. Not now.

She raised her head and pulled back. "I don't have to worry about telling him anymore."

"What did you want to tell him?" Nate asked, compassion overriding any other feeling.

In a voice barely above a whisper she said, "I'm pregnant.''

ONE

The grumble of thunder penetrated Nate's air-conditioned office as the driving rain beat at the west-facing windows. A grip of uneasiness twisted his stomach and he reached for the telephone. There was a rap on the door a second before it opened.

Nate's hand slipped off the receiver as he looked up to see Jerry Winslow, his editor-in-chief. "How bad is it?"

"Same as yesterday. Severe thunderstorm warnings until eight P.M. This is some June we're having."

Nate glanced at the phone again. He didn't want Shara to think he was checking up on her. For the last eight months, he had tried to be supportive, had tried to be available without being intrusive, had tried to keep his thoughts and feelings to himself while he encouraged her friendship. She hadn't talked to Nate about Jim's death, but he'd watched her work through the stages and come to an acceptance.

Maybe her pregnancy had helped with that. She had

another life to consider and she needed to move on. But was she ready to move on to him? And if she was, what did he want? An affair? A relationship? More? He cherished his freedom to stay, to pick up and go when he pleased without answering to anyone.

"Nate," Jerry said impatiently, mowing his hand through his receding brown hair.

Nate's head jerked up. "What?"

"I asked if you're going to leave early."

"Are the streets flooding?"

"Some of them." Jerry sighed heavily. "What's on your mind?"

"I should call Shara. But I don't want her to think—"

"That you care? She's got to know that by now." Nate's gray eyes must have shown his alarm because Jerry soothed, "I don't mean like that. She knows you'll help if she needs help."

Nate stared out the window, trying to see through the storm. "She's independent. She doesn't want to lean on anybody, and I'm afraid she won't call me if she needs someone. The false labor pains she's been having all week have made her hesitant to phone her doctor or go to the hospital." He closed the folder on his desk and pushed it aside. "Why do I want to help her so badly? Is it because I'm the one who told her her husband was dead?"

Jerry came closer to Nate's desk. "Why were you first attracted to her?"

"I don't know." Nate closed his eyes for a moment to answer the question for himself. He gave up trying and stared at his editor. "I just know the day she walked into my office, I knew she was special. So damn pretty, her voice soft . . ."

Jerry hitched his trousers higher on his hips. "There are a lot of women out there who are pretty."

Nate began shaking his head before Jerry was finished. "It's more than that. I like her—really like her. She's intelligent, compassionate—"

"And a widow who was planning to get a divorce before she became a widow," Jerry stuck in. "Don't you think it's time you made your move?"

Nate gave the editor a sideways glance. "All she thinks and talks about is this baby. And right now, I don't want her alone out there in a storm."

"A phone call can't hurt."

Jerry wasn't merely Nate's editor, he was a good friend. Three years ago when Nate purchased the defunct *Herald*, he'd needed someone talented and capable who was willing to settle in York, Pennsylvania. Jerry had been that person. Together they'd turned the paper around and made it thrive.

Nate knew Jerry had watched his attraction for Shara grow during the few weeks she'd worked with the newspaper's employees, demonstrating techniques to handle stress. She'd been separated from her husband at the time. Nate had known better than to get involved with a woman who wasn't divorced. When he'd seen Shara a few weeks later and through polite conversation discovered she and her husband were getting a divorce, his heart had soared and he knew he would bide his time. He'd never anticipated Nolan's recklessness.

After the baby was born, maybe she could start a new life. A sour thought hit him. Or maybe she still wouldn't want a man in her life. Maybe her son or daughter would require all of her time and attention.

Nate snapped his attention back to the present, took his

friend's advice, and picked up the receiver. He punched Shara's number and waited, his brows drawing together in frustration. "It's busy."

Jerry sat with one hip lodged on the corner of Nate's desk. "So give her a couple of minutes."

"What is it, Jerry?" Nate asked, studying his editor carefully. The man was rarely still, always restless, incessantly working. Enforced calm meant something.

"Bloomfield called again. Since you turned down his offer to buy back the paper, he thought he'd work on me. He offered me a healthy raise if I could convince you to sell."

Nate's eyes grew stormy. "That's why he went bankrupt last time. He made promises he couldn't keep."

"I told him I wasn't interested unless you were." Jerry thrummed his fingers on the desk. "I figured you might get tired of this soon. If you do, maybe I'll stay, maybe I'll move on, too."

As a photojournalist, Nate had traveled and seen places that were war-torn, under siege, buried in mud, under threat of a volcano blowing sky high. He was good at what he did. His services were in demand by national publications. For now, dangerous assignments were a side course, not his main diet, but he never knew what the future would bring.

"I don't intend to sell the paper for a year or two anyway," he said.

Jerry's brows drew together. "You've taken more assignments since Nolan died, almost one a month. Want to tell me why that is?"

"They came up. I want to stay fresh."

"You're as fresh as a rosebud and you know it. Maybe

it has something to do with facing your own mortality? Or maybe facing what you feel about Shara?''

"Since when did you hang out a shingle?'' Nate snapped. He hadn't stopped to think about his reasons, but now that he did, Jerry was right on both counts. And both counts unnerved him.

"No shingle. Just calling it like I see it. The idea of settling down makes some men run long and hard. You one of them?''

"Settling down isn't the problem. Feeling trapped is.''

"What makes you feel trapped?''

"Responsibility closing in on me. I know what it's like, Jerry. When I was ten, my father left me, my mother, and my kid brother. From then on I knew what responsibility was. I was the man of the house. I not only took out the garbage, I ran errands and took whatever jobs I could get to help pay the bills. It wasn't until a couple of years out of college that I finally felt free to live my life. Brad was on his own. I bought Mom a house in a retirement village and her life was stable. I vowed I'd never feel trapped again.''

"So you chase thrills to prove you're free.''

"No. I do what I love to do, photograph what I want to photograph. Any place. Any time.''

"Did you ever consider that feeling trapped might simply be a state of mind?''

Nate's shoulders stiffened defensively. "Give me a break! Being tied down to one place isn't in the mind.''

"Being tied down to one woman?''

Enough was enough, even from a friend. Jerry's questions were making him uncomfortable. Nate scowled, scooped up the receiver again, and jabbed Shara's number. When he heard the busy signal, he swore and slapped down the phone. "That's it. I'm going to see if she's all right." And the consequences be damned.

Nate stood up, threw an "I'll be back later" over his shoulder, and was out the door before Jerry could blink. He heard his editor mutter, "You forgot your umbrella."

As a contraction ripped through Shara, she threw her arms across her abdomen and leaned against the living-room wall for support. It was the second one in less than ten minutes and it was awful. She held in her breath and waited. Hot wetness trickled down her legs and was caught in her socks. Her water had broken. This wasn't the false labor she had been having all week. This wasn't the cramping that would go away in an hour.

Taking a bolstering breath, Shara gingerly walked to the gossip bench. She lowered herself slowly and picked up the phone. There was no tone. It was dead. As she stood up, another contraction began and swelled. She didn't have a watch but guessed the pains were three minutes apart. She needed help . . . and fast.

When the contraction subsided, she headed for the door. "All I have to do is keep calm. It's after five. Amber could be home."

Shara opened the door and couldn't believe her eyes. As she peered through the sheets of rain, she saw the street was flooded. Water bubbled over the curbs. Wind slapped her with rain. Although she merely had to get to Amber's side of the duplex, she was drenched by the time she reached her next-door neighbor's bell. She jabbed again and again but knew it was hopeless. Amber had probably gotten stuck at work.

Shara had just reached the safety of her own doorway when another contraction hit. She doubled over and panted, trying to float through the pain. "Labor is labor, girl. You learned that in the Peace Corps when you helped women deliver their babies. Many of them did it alone. You can do it alone. For God's sake, don't panic."

When the contraction ended, Shara hurried to the kitchen, knowing her time was limited to three-minute intervals. She managed to flick off her sneakers, bend over, and unlace the shoestrings.

"Versatile, innovative—that's what I am. If I keep talking to myself, maybe I won't be so scared that I'm doing this alone. A hysterical woman is no good to anyone. Certainly not to a newborn baby. It could be morning 'til the phone's repaired." A sob caught in her throat. "Easy, Shara. Take it easy."

As she pulled a small saucepan from her cupboard, another contraction tightened. She panted through it and tried to keep the tears behind her eyes. If she let them loose, she'd break down. She couldn't do that.

After she caught her breath, she put water on to boil and dropped the shoelaces and pair of scissors into the pot. Quickly pulling out of the drawer as many towels as she could find, she went to the living room and spread them on the sofa. The sharpness of the next contraction bent her over and she collapsed on the cushion. She opened her mouth and took short, shallow breaths.

When she could think again, she said aloud, "Amber, you might be my Lamaze coach, but we're going to see if I absorbed your part in all this, too. I have to take this pain by pain, watch the signs, keep cool and—" Shara's voice shook. "If you don't come home soon, deliver this baby myself."

Two minutes later when a pain stabbed her again, a lone tear rolled down her cheek. Amber was her best friend. Shara wanted her here. Who else could help? The face that flashed in front of her eyes startled her. It was Nate's. Why would she think of him when this was happening? Because for the past eight months he'd been a caring influence. Strength surrounded him. Confidence led him. God, how she needed both right now.

Nate drove his Ford Econoline van carefully, very carefully, through the flooded streets. A slash of lightning streaked across the sky. As the windshield wipers struggled to clear the windows, he prayed the van wouldn't stall out. It had never let him down, but there was always a first time. When he turned into Shara's street, he heaved a sigh of relief. He pulled into her driveway, set the emergency brake, and jumped out. Knocking hard on the door, he didn't wait for an answer but turned the knob and pushed the door open.

He swiped the rain from his brow and saw Shara hunched up on the sofa, her knees drawn up as far as she could manage. In two long strides he was beside her. "I knew it," he said grimly, panic making his chest tighten.

She looked at him as if he were a mirage, someone conjured up by her imagination. But as water dripped from his arm onto her hand, she realized he was real. "The baby's coming, Nate. The phone's dead and I'm scared."

Her hair was wet; her cotton blouse molded to her breasts. Her shorts were dropped by the side of the sofa and she had draped an afghan over her lap.

"Shara, you need an ambulance. Maybe one of your neighbors will have phone service or a CB or something. I'll go try—"

She grabbed his hand and squeezed hard. "No, Nate.

Don't leave, please. It'll take too much time and I need you here.''

Nate remembered rappeling down an icy cliff. He remembered feeling the rope jerk, his fear it was tearing. That fear was nothing compared to this. Could he help deliver Shara's baby? There were so many consequences to consider. They ran through his mind at the speed of light.

What if something went wrong? What if the baby was turned or in the wrong position? Even if the delivery went smoothly, how would Shara feel if he saw her naked? If he experienced the pain with her? If he had to see and touch her intimately? Wouldn't she be embarrassed? Wouldn't he? Wouldn't she regret it later? Wouldn't she try to forget everything and keep him at a distance because he saw too much?

With a blinding insight he realized he wanted to get closer to this woman. As soon as the thought formed, he heard the bars of a cage rattle and a voice inside his head shouted, ''What happens to your freedom if you do?''

Shara moaned and Nate knew he had no choice but to help deliver this baby. He had to get some sense of where they were in the birthing process. ''Okay, Shara. This is going to be a piece of cake,'' he soothed, as much to himself as to her.

''For you maybe.''

He chuckled, glad to see her spunk hadn't deserted her. ''This is a natural process. Think of the millions of women in sterile hospital rooms who just wish they had the chance to have their baby at home.''

''This is not my fondest wish, Nate. Heaven knows a sterile hospital room would look awfully good . . .''

As Nate saw the contraction beginning, he pulled down

the afghan slightly and placed his hand on Shara's abdomen just above her navel. He could feel the hardness of the contraction. It lasted sixty seconds.

Shara took deep breaths with her mouth open. When she could speak, she said, "They're two minutes apart."

He tugged his tie loose and threw it onto the recliner next to the sofa. "You don't mess around, do you?" He wanted to scold her for not calling someone when labor started, he wanted to yell at her for looking so damned beautiful even though she was wet and in pain, he wanted to scream, *Why have you put me in this position?* But he didn't.

It took a strong mental effort for him to keep his face calm. "Tell me where you keep your clean sheets and robe so you can get out of those wet clothes before you catch pneumonia."

"Sheets are in the linen closet at the top of the stairs. My robe's on the bedroom chair."

Nate saw naked fear in Shara's green eyes. He sandwiched her hand between his. "Shara, if it's any consolation, I've done this before. My brother Brad was born at home. I watched. I remember the midwife telling me and Dad there was nothing to fear. She said if we didn't hurry and we let nature take its course, everything would be fine. When I was in Ethiopia covering the famine, I helped a mother deliver by the side of the road. The delivery was the easy part."

Shara's eyes asked why and Nate answered, "I held that baby and I saw no hope for his future. Not only wouldn't he have the medical attention he would need, but he wouldn't even have enough food. You're lucky, Shara. From the moment your baby's born, he'll have hope."

Shara squeezed his palm. "Thanks. That helps me keep this in perspective."

Her bright eyes, her brave smile, made him want to take her in his arms and protect her. But he couldn't do that. He released her hand. "I'll be right back."

When he returned with the sheets and robe, Shara was in the throes of another contraction. The catch of her breath revealed the extent of the pain she sought to control. He knew what the effort cost her. He had seen soldiers hit in guerilla warfare swallow screams when they'd been injured. He knew the terror that came with intense pain.

"Don't hold it in, Shara. Certainly not on my account."

She ignored his suggestion and gasped, "It's changing. Instead of the tightness and pain across my back, I feel a bearing-down sensation. The baby's moving down."

Nate glanced at the pot of water on the floor next to Shara. The scissors would cut the cord. The shoelaces would be used to tie it off. She'd thought of everything, and she would have delivered this baby herself. He swallowed the lump in his throat and asked huskily, "Can you slip off your blouse?"

Shara's fingers fumbled as she unfastened the buttons. Nate turned away and she was glad he had. For some unknown, ridiculous reason, she was seeing him as a man, more than a friend. She was about to have a baby, and she was concerned about Nate seeing her body and not liking what he saw. How stupid could she get? It must be the pain clouding her sensibilities. Until they were done here, he was going to see more than her breasts.

Once she removed her bra, she tried to shift into her robe, but the movement was impossible. So she put on the garment backward like a hospital gown. "Okay," she croaked hoarsely.

When Nate turned around, his lips twitched with amusement. "New style?"

"I always wanted to be a trendsetter." As Nate arranged a sheet on top of her and pulled off the heavy afghan, she studied his face. It wasn't traditionally handsome. It had lines and crags and bushy brows that gave him a fierce expression until he smiled. Then his eyes sparkled with gray light and his features softened.

Nate's face swam into a blur as Shara felt another contraction begin. She panted loudly.

He crouched down beside her, held her hand and said, "Thatta girl. You're going to be able to tell the women of America how easy home births can be."

She struggled through the cramping, trying not to scream.

"Don't be a stoic, Shara. Let it go. If you want to yell, yell. You'll feel better."

"I can't yell," she flared. "I have to breathe."

He smiled. "What can I do to help?"

"Remind me to breathe." Her voice wheezed into a squeal that lasted to the end of the contraction. She gulped in air. "Nate, I've been trying not to push. I didn't think it was time. But it feels like I should."

His wavy black hair slipped down his forehead when he raised his head, and his tanned cheeks were flushed. "I'm going to have to examine you and see how far along you are. Okay?"

She bit her lower lip and nodded. Pulling her knees up, she separated her legs.

He didn't touch her. Just looked. He put the sheet back in place and knelt beside her. "From what I can tell, I think you're fully dilated.'' He wiped her damp hair away from her brow. "It won't be long now. I'm going to help you scoot down closer to the end of the sofa so you can prop your feet on the arm. That way I can get better leverage, and when the baby's born, I can support him on my arms and hands.''

"This is really happening, Nate, isn't it? It's not a dream. In not too long, I'm going to have a baby in my arms.''

"And in your heart.''

Shara looked at Nate with wonder. He understood. He really understood. Because of his brother?

The moment was shattered by the tightening of her muscles, then relief during a brief period of relaxation. It happened over and over again until she wondered if this would ever end. Every time she weathered a contraction, she told herself they couldn't get any worse. But each one topped the one before.

Nate helped her move farther down the sofa and made her as comfortable as he could with pillows. But the tension on his face reflected her pain as he coached her in breathing.

Shara was beginning to wonder whether this baby would ever be born when she saw Nate grin and heard him say joyously, "I can see the top of the head! When the next contraction comes, push but listen to me.''

She knew if she pushed too hard, too fast, she'd tear. He knew it, too. As the next contraction swept over her, she pushed.

"It's coming. Stop pushing.''

"I can't.''

"Sure you can. Pant through it. C'mon. Pant.''

She panted—as if her life depended on it. He kept calm.

"There's no hurry about this. Take it easy. Nice and slow."

"Nate, I want to push."

His voice was deep, laced with an authority that was comforting. "Slowly. Slowly. I know you can do this. It's better for you and the baby to go slowly. Think of the baby, concentrate on your breathing."

As the pain diminished and she laid her head back to catch her breath, Nate gave directions. "Okay. Now with the next contraction, bear down. Easy."

The pain scorched her insides, twisted, wrenched, turned. Shara was swirling in a spiral of pain, excitement, longing, and joy. The pushing sapped her strength and she gasped when she had to let go of the effort.

The force of her push seemed to surge through Nate. His eyes said he ached to help her, but he wasn't sure how. So he encouraged. "Easy, Shara. Easy. C'mon, the shoulders are out. One more giant push."

Her cheeks hot, her face dripping with perspiration from the exertion, Shara gave the monumental effort he asked for. Just as she thought she was going to faint from the ordeal, she heard a cry. She looked up at Nate. Their gazes locked and held for an everlasting moment.

Nate wrapped a towel around the baby and laid the child on his side on Shara's abdomen. "You have a son, Shara. An exquisite son."

Her baby was red, wrinkled, wriggling . . . and real. As she brought her arms around him and stared, her tears finally fell. When she looked from her son back to Nate, she saw the same wetness on his face. They had shared a miracle.

TWO

As director of Health Promotion at York Community Hospital, Shara had many friends at the institution, so when she was admitted, she was treated like a royal guest. She was given the best room on the maternity floor at the end of the hall, away from the hustle and bustle of the nurses' desk.

The day following her son's birth, Shara ate a last spoonful of pudding and was pushing her lunch tray to the side when Nate walked into the room—tall, broad-shouldered, a lopsided smile curving his lips. He was carrying a bouquet of yellow sweetheart roses.

"Hi," he said tentatively, crossing to the bed.

"Hi," she returned shyly, remembering how he had gently massaged her abdomen as they waited for the afterbirth, remembering him expertly tying and cutting the cord, remembering the awesome moment they'd shared when her son was born.

She took the bull by the horns. "Are you as embarrassed as I am?"

A look of relief passed over his face. "Now, what do we have to be embarrassed about? Man of the world that I am, delivering babies is all in a day's work."

Nate's blue shirt was a soft material, fitting loosely. But it hinted at the outline of muscle underneath. The khaki slacks were casual. His demeanor was relaxed, but his eyes weren't. Because of the experience they had shared? Probably. Her eyes lowered to his hands still holding the flowers. Those strong, capable hands had delivered her baby.

"I don't know how to thank you, Nate. I don't know what I would have done."

He laid the bouquet on the table next to her lunch tray and sat down on the chair next to the bed. "You would've done fine. I happened to be there to help. How are you feeling?"

He was a good friend, making her feel comfortable when the situation could be very awkward. "I'm a little sore." She felt smears of heat suffuse her cheeks because he knew exactly why. Her eyes met his. "But the doctor says I'm fine and so is Danny."

"Daniel's his name?"

"Uh huh. Daniel *Nathan* Nolan." She watched Nate's expression as understanding dawned and he realized she'd bestowed on the baby his given name.

"You didn't have to do that."

"I wanted to."

Nate ran his hand through his hair, ruffling it. "When he was born, when I held him in my hands, I felt as if he were part mine." A peculiar expression passed over Shara's face and Nate apologized. "Shara, I'm sorry. I didn't mean to make it sound . . ."

"It's okay, Nate. I know what you mean."

Nate mentally kicked himself. What a stupid thing to say, even if it was true. Time to change the subject. "Are you going to have any help when you go home?"

"Amber's going to stay with me a few nights. I don't know what I'd do without her. You've never met her, have you?"

"No, but you talk about her as if you're as close as sisters."

"We are. We're so different, but somehow we fit together."

"Differences add spice to friendships."

"Friends usually share the same interests. The only thing Amber and I have in common is that we're neighbors."

"What makes you friends?"

Shara thought about it for a moment. "We like each other an awful lot. Amber's zany, but I can always count on her."

Shara's hand was only a few inches from his on top of the covers. He wanted to take it in his, but he didn't have that freedom. "Your parents aren't coming?"

"They're in England."

Something in her voice said this was a controversial subject so he didn't pry. "At least you won't have to worry about someone taking over. Mom wanted to help Brad and his wife decorate their nursery. She ended up doing it singlehandedly. Luckily, Brad's wife is very easy-going and didn't resent it. But Brad gave Mom a lecture that lasted a week."

Shara pushed her long hair behind her ear. "Where does your family live?"

"Raleigh, North Carolina."

"You were born there?"

Nate's spirits lifted a mile. During the eight months he'd tried to become Shara's friend, they hadn't exchanged background information. If she was interested in his past, she might be interested in him.

He grinned. "I was born there, but Brad says I'm rootless. He says anyone who's traveled as much as I have, calls the world his home, not one town."

"Is that the way it is?"

More than casual interest was on her face. At least that's the way he wanted to read it. "It used to be. Since I bought the paper, I feel York's home. Maybe it's because I bought a house, too. Real estate makes a man feel he belongs somewhere."

Shara agreed with Nate. She'd wanted a house. But Jim hadn't. He'd complained he didn't have time for the upkeep. Life was much simpler when a landlord cut the grass and took care of weatherstripping. Why would she think of Jim now? And why would she compare him to Nate? She looked back at Nate. She'd heard rumors about him, the chances he'd taken, the places he'd been. But it sounded like his life of globe-trotting was over and he'd decided to plant roots.

"What are you thinking about?" Nate asked.

"Lots of things," she evaded. "The differences between people mainly."

He smiled. "Those thoughts are too philosophical for a day like this. Have you looked out the window? It's a beautiful day—turquoise sky, puffy clouds, enough sun to make flash cubes obsolete."

"A photographer's dream?"

"Photographers have many dreams."

Shara looked into his eyes and saw something different. They were usually gentle and friendly. But now there was something else. Something that caused a ripple of excitement to skip up her spine.

The feeling made her nervous and her hands fluttered as she spoke. "Do you want to go see Danny? I could use the stretch."

"Sure." He stood up, looking unsure. "Do you need help?"

She smiled. "No, I'm fine. Would you hand me my robe?"

He picked up the blue nylon garment he'd brought her when she was in labor. "Your nightgown matches. How did you get it?"

"Amber brought my suitcase this morning. In the excitement last night, I forgot all about it." She donned the robe before she slipped out from between the sheets, stood up, and stepped into her moccasins.

Nate matched his pace to hers, all the while aware of the clinging nightgown and robe. He remembered the pure whiteness of her skin, its softness, its suppleness. For the first time in eight months he let himself imagine touching it, not as a caregiver, but as a lover. Yet as soon as he saw the picture in his mind, he blanked it out. This woman was a new mother. He shouldn't be thinking in terms of fantasies.

When they arrived at the large window at the nursery, Shara smiled and tears brightened her eyes. "Isn't he beautiful, Nate? Isn't he absolutely beautiful?"

Nate couldn't prevent his arm from dropping across Shara's shoulders. Daniel Nathan Nolan was perfect in every way. From the thatch of scraggly brown hair on his head to the fist he was trying to shove into his mouth. An intense feeling of protectiveness gripped Nate. He wanted this child to have every advantage—to want for nothing.

And the baby's mother? He stopped the thoughts before he could think them.

Nate kept his voice matter of fact. "Shara, if you need anything, if Danny needs anything, don't hesitate to call me."

Shara turned to Nate and seemed to sense the bond between him and the child. She smiled. "We'll be fine."

"I know you're taking a three-month leave of absence from the hospital. Are you set financially?"

"We're okay until September. I wish I could stay home longer, but I'll have three months to find a good baby-sitter."

Nate leaned back from the nursery window and looked down at her. "I was thinking. Since your specialty is disease prevention through stress control and nutrition, maybe you could do a series of articles for our health column."

Her green eyes held his steadily. "You don't have to do that."

"Do what? Find an expert who can intelligently tell the public how to stay well?"

"What will your editor say if *you* choose the columnist?" Her voice was accusing.

Nate lifted one shoulder in a half shrug. "He'll agree you're the person for the job. Remember, Jerry saw you work with our staff. You're good."

"Maybe I can't write."

"Shara . . ."

She ignored his warning tone. "I don't want charity, Nate."

He took his arm away from her shoulders and faced her squarely. "Shara Nolan, don't be obstinate. If what you write is of no earthly use, I'll toss it in the circular file.

If it has merit and it's well written, I'll print it. Understand?''

She looked surprised by his forcefulness but seemed to decide he was telling the truth. "All right. Under those conditions, I'll give it a try."

"Good." He gave her a hard look. "We understand each other. Now, let's go back to the room before you tire yourself out."

"You're as bad as Amber. She said the same thing this morning."

He grinned but didn't comment as he accompanied her back to her room.

Shara slid into bed and covered herself with the sheet. "I guess you have to go back to work."

He wanted to stay and talk to her, but the same attraction that drew him to her was pushing him away. He told himself she looked tired, that she needed her rest before she went home and had to care for a baby full time.

"Yes, I do. Jerry's great, but there are some problems he can't handle."

"You and he are good friends."

"We go back a long way. We understand each other." Too well.

"How can you be friends when you're the boss?"

"Bruce Springsteen's 'the boss.' I merely own the newspaper."

She laughed—a wonderful, musical sound. "False modesty?"

"No modesty. Realistic awareness. The paper wouldn't be successful without Jerry. We both know it."

A nurse pushed open the door and stepped into the room. When she saw Nate, her eyes widened with approval. "Is this the man who delivered Danny?"

"Sure is, Wanda. But he's probably too modest to take the credit."

Nate liked Shara's ability to joke even though he was the butt of it. "Guilty as charged."

Wanda peeked into Shara's water pitcher and found it icy and full. "I heard you did a good job—better than some of our doctors." She looked at Shara. "You're a lucky lady. There's a reporter waiting in the lounge if you want to talk to him."

"Not from my paper," Nate assured.

Shara appeared agitated. "Wanda, can you get rid of him? I don't want my life in print. Unless . . . Nate?"

He shook his head vigorously. "No way. I don't want the publicity, either. I'll get rid of him when I leave."

Wanda stuck a thermometer in Shara's mouth, cuffed her arm, and took her blood pressure. When she was finished she said to Nate, "I'll tell the guy you'll talk to him."

"How's she doing?" Nate asked before he thought better of it.

"Just fine. She'll probably be going home day after tomorrow. The problem is she has too many friends in this hospital and we have to make sure she gets enough time to herself."

Nate took that as a hint. He shook his finger at Shara. "You behave yourself. If you want to sleep, tell the company to leave."

She saluted. "Yes, sir."

He stood at the bottom of the bed, wanting to kiss her, needing to touch her, but too confused by his feelings to do either. In a safe, comforting gesture, he patted her foot beneath the sheet. "Take care of yourself. I'll be in touch."

After another of Shara's "thank you's," Nate left the room feeling as if he was leaving some part of himself behind. But that was impossible. Leaving had never been a problem. Why should it be now?

Amber Selinski yelled up Shara's steps. "Do you have any coasters? My glass of iced tea is sweating all over your coffee table and I don't want to ruin the maple finish."

Shara appeared at the top of the steps, her crying son on her shoulder. Danny was wearing a diaper and rubber pants, Shara a red knit top with spaghetti straps and white shorts. Much to her delight, her prepregnancy clothes fit. She had watched her diet and started sit-ups a week after she delivered Danny. She corrected herself. A week after she *and Nate* had delivered Danny. She had three more pounds she wanted to lose. That shouldn't be a problem in this heat with a new baby demanding her time and attention.

Shara patted Danny's bare, sticky back and crooned to him softly as she descended the stairs into the comfortably furnished living room. The furniture was Early American, upholstered in gold and green flowers. The brown corduroy recliner had already seen many hours of rocking a fussy baby.

Danny quieted but moved restively against Shara's shoulder as she pointed to the end table in answer to Amber's question. "Coasters are in that drawer."

"How long did he sleep?" Amber dashed her hand across the side of her cheek to swipe away a bead of perspiration. Her hand continued upward and her long maroon fingernails swept through her short, curly red hair that had frizzed in the high humidity.

When Shara sat down in the recliner, her three-week-old son began crying again. Even though it was evening, the heat hadn't lessened. Standing, she paced around the room. "Twenty minutes. I don't know what to do. He needs sleep. I need sleep. With the air-conditioning broken, I don't know how we're going to get it. The fans don't help. I'm seriously thinking about going to the mall for a few hours so he can be comfortable and nap."

"It's just our luck it's the weekend before the Fourth of July and the serviceman can't get the part he needs. I don't know how you're doing it. Have you gotten any sleep the last two nights?" Amber took a coaster out of the drawer in the end table, put it under her glass, and crossed one darkly tanned leg over the other.

"I've been napping whenever he does, but he's not sleeping long enough at one time."

Amber swung her leg back and forth. "According to your charts, you should experience an upswing this month. Hold on to that to get you through the heat."

Amber, a paralegal secretary, dabbled in astrology. Shara knew she firmly believed in its accuracy and use in daily life. Amber had tried to make Shara a believer, but Shara was skeptical. "You consult your charts and I'll put my faith in the repairman."

Sitting down on the recliner again, she pushed with her foot to rock Danny. He seemed content for the moment. Her eyes drifted up to the half dozen, helium-filled balloons bobbing against the corner of the ceiling. She smiled.

Amber must have followed the direction of her friend's gaze because she asked, "Has Nate stopped by yet?"

"No. He just keeps sending things every few days.

Yesterday a messenger brought a baseball glove and ball. When I wrote him a note to thank him—"

Taking advantage of their four years of friendship, Amber boldly cut in. "Why didn't you call him?"

Shara had asked herself the same question. She hadn't found the answer. "He's probably busy. It just seemed easier—"

"Easier or safer?" Amber interrupted again.

Shara rocked faster. "I don't know what you mean."

"Sure, you do. You simply don't want to admit it. When you and Jim were separated and you worked with Nate, you said you liked him."

"Well, of course I did. He was friendly and pleasant."

"And after Jim died, he called you often to make sure you were okay."

Shara pulled Danny's rubber pants up a little higher. "So did other people."

With her usual directness, Amber continued. "And toward the end of your pregnancy, he called you once a week to make sure you didn't need anything."

Shara glanced sideways at the redhead. "Did you have my phone tapped?"

Amber giggled. "No, I did not. You volunteered the information freely, whether you knew it or not, because you were glad he cared."

"What's this leading up to?" Shara asked warily, guessing Amber was set on making a point.

Amber shrugged her shoulders and drained her iced tea. After she put the glass down, she concluded, "A man doesn't go to all that trouble for nothing."

Telling herself Nate was merely being kind and considerate, Shara hadn't looked for hidden motives. But that day in the hospital, something had changed between them. She hadn't taken the time to analyze what it was.

As much to herself as to Amber, she said, "Nate's a friend."

Amber stood. "Umm hmm. A friend. The next time you talk to him, find out the date, year, and time of his birth and where he was born. I want to do his chart."

"Amber—"

Amber held up her hand like a stop sign. "Don't give me a lot of flak, just get it." Before Shara could object, her friend started for the door. "While you were upstairs, I wrote down Leon's phone number and address and put it on your refrigerator. I'm sleeping there until the aircon-ditioning's fixed. If you need me, that's where I'll be. I'd ask you and Danny to come with me, but Leon's apart-ment is small and we bump elbows as it is."

Amber and Leon had been dating for two years. Although Amber was two years Shara's senior at thirty-two, she'd told Shara she wasn't ready to make a commit-ment to him. She was content to snatch time with Leon whenever she could, make no demands on him, and put off making a decision about their future. Shara couldn't understand that type of relationship. But then maybe she'd always wanted too much.

"You don't mind a bit," Shara said with confidence.

"Nope," Amber agreed. "Listen, Shara, why don't I lend you the money for an air conditioner? You can take as long as you want to pay me back."

"Thanks for offering, but we'll be okay. This heat has to break soon. You enjoy the holiday with Leon. Tell him I said hi."

"Will do. I'll see you when I get back."

The bang of the screen door as Amber left startled

Danny and he began crying. Shara jiggled him, and when that didn't help, she shifted him to her other shoulder. That was no better. She couldn't sink money she didn't have into an air conditioner that she might only need for a few days. She had to save as much money as she could so she could stay home an additional month with Danny.

She looked down at her hot, disgruntled son. Maybe if she gave him a bottle, he'd slip into sleep. Shara went to the kitchen to heat one in the microwave. By the time the oven beeped, Danny was crying at the top of his lungs. When Shara opened the door to the oven, her doorbell rang. She shifted her son to the crook of her arm, reached for the bottle, and went to answer the door.

Nate stood on the porch, looking sexier than any man had a right to look.

THREE

Shara didn't know whether to be pleased or dismayed to see Nate standing there. Knowing she couldn't be heard over the baby's crying, she motioned for him to come in. When he did, he took Danny from her and cradled the baby in his arm. Danny stopped crying. Nate dragged a finger down the infant's chest in a caressing touch. Danny found Nate's finger and held tightly.

Shara marveled at Nate's gentleness and sensitivity. She had never seen a man show so much caring with one small gesture. Why was he so comfortable with a baby? Most men were afraid of them.

She smiled. "I don't believe it. I've been jiggling, rocking, swaying, and walking to quiet him, and all you have to do is pick him up!"

Nate's grin was smug. "We men know how to relate."

Shara shook her head in exasperation as her eyes took in Nate's appearance. He looked different. Denim shorts instead of tailored slacks. A polo shirt instead of a dress shirt. Sneakers with frayed laces instead of soft leather shoes. He looked so . . . so male!

"Is something wrong?" Nate asked when he saw her staring.

"No . . . I . . ." She felt flustered and said the first words that came to mind. "How dare you look like that on a day like this?"

His eyes twinkled with amusement. "How am I supposed to look?"

"You're supposed to look hot, bothered, and miserable like everyone else. If I could run around nude . . . I mean, clothes make you so much hotter, but I can't run around like that on the first floor with the windows open . . ." Her cheeks grew red with spots of color and she stopped before she made matters worse.

As Nate's gaze swept from her flushed cheeks, over white shoulders untouched by the summer sun, down her long legs and bare feet, he wasn't miserable, but if he looked too long, he could become hot and bothered. He was startled by the desire that bit him. Danny became restless in his arm and began crying.

Shifting his stance, Nate nodded at the bottle. "Can I do that?"

A soft, fragile look came into Shara's eyes. "Sure. If you sit in the recliner, you can rock. He likes that."

After he and the baby were settled, Nate gazed down at Danny, startled by the tenderness, unnerved by the attachment he felt. When he looked up at Shara, he saw dark circles under her eyes. She looked frazzled. He'd wanted to come visit sooner, but had told himself it was better for her if he didn't, that she needed time to adjust. But he'd wanted to see and hold this child he had helped bring into the world. At least that's what he told himself.

So he'd turned his back on his better judgment and here he was.

As Danny sucked rhythmically on the bottle, Nate asked, "How are you making out in this heat?"

Shara curled her legs under her on the sofa. "The air-conditioning system broke down. It won't be fixed until Tuesday because of the holiday. So we're battling it the best we can."

"And neither of you are sleeping," Nate deduced.

A stray strand of hair stuck to Shara's cheek when she leaned forward. She brushed it back. "Something like that."

Several ideas crossed Nate's mind. Shara wasn't a complainer, and he knew she wouldn't accept an extravagant solution like letting him put her in a hotel suite for a few days. He had to offer something reasonable. "The van's air-conditioned. Let me take you for a long drive. Maybe Danny will sleep and you can relax."

Doubt crossed her face. "I don't know."

"You have a car seat for him, don't you?" Nate coaxed.

"Yes. I could put a knit shirt and booties on him so he doesn't get chilled in the van." She warmed to the idea. "He does need the sleep."

"Yep. And you need a respite. Grab some diapers and another bottle and we'll get going. Don't worry about Danny. I know how to burp."

Shara's eyes found Nate's. "You're a nice man, Nate McKendrick."

He smiled wryly, supposing "nice" was as good a start as any.

As Nate drove through York County countryside, the farmland rolled by. Corn fields were knee-high, and with all the rain they had been getting, the grassland was a rich green.

Nate caught Shara taking a third quick glance at Danny in the seat behind him. "He's fine, Shara."

She sighed and relaxed in her bucket seat. "I guess the worrying will never stop now that I'm a parent. Sometimes when he's sleeping, I put my hand on his back to make sure he's breathing. Does that mean I'm going to be overprotective?"

"I think you're intuitive enough to know when to be protective and when not to be."

Nate always seemed to know the right thing to say. "Thank you for all the goodies you sent this week. I'll appreciate the box of imported chocolates as much as Danny will appreciate the rattles. Did you get my notes?"

"Every one of them. But they weren't necessary."

"A lady always writes a thank-you note for a gift."

"Says who?"

"Mrs. Pennington."

"And who is Mrs. Pennington?"

"She was my nanny."

Nate glanced at her out of the corner of his eye. "You had *that* kind of childhood? You don't seem the type."

"What type?"

"You're down to earth, practical, you don't expect others to do what you can do for yourself."

He had her pegged. He seemed to know her a lot better than she knew him. "I've always been that way. Mrs. Pennington called it being self-willed. I was never sure if it was a compliment or a putdown."

"Definitely a compliment. How long did you have a nanny?"

"Until I went to boarding school."

Nate shook his head. "Was that your choice?"

"Heavens, no. My stepfather decided it was the only way to get a proper education." She didn't tell Nate the real reason. Her stepfather didn't want her around. He didn't want to raise a child. He wanted a wife who looked good on his arm, who could impress his business associates with her youthfulness. He didn't want a family.

"How did you like it?"

She hated it. She'd wanted a family like the kind in books or on TV. A mother, father, brothers and sisters. People who wanted to be together, who loved each other. "I received an excellent education. But most of the time I was . . . lonely."

Nate looked at her as if he wanted to say something, but he didn't. He switched on his left-turn signal and slowed the van. When Shara looked across the road, she saw a stand that served soft ice cream. Picnic tables were scattered along the sides of the building.

"Hungry for ice cream?" Nate asked with a boyish expression that said he knew this place well.

"Is ice cream one of your weaknesses?" Her curiosity was piqued about a man who was a world traveler but could still enjoy a treat as simple as an ice-cream cone.

He turned into the gravel parking lot, braked, and switched off the ignition. "If I tell you the truth, will you promise not to hold it against me?"

His tone was playful and brought out a like response in Shara. "It might cost you."

His gray eyes played with her green ones. "You aren't capable of blackmail."

"You don't know my alter ego." She grinned, thinking how good it felt to laugh and talk with Nate.

"I'd like to," he said quietly, the playful tint gone from his words.

Shara sat very still. Her heart accelerated and she wondered if she was placing too much importance on a single statement. Amber's voice echoed clearly. *A man doesn't go to all that trouble for nothing.* Was Nate being more than friendly? And if he was, was she ready? More important, didn't she have a baby to consider?

He must have read the confusion in her eyes. Reaching across the gear shift to her seat, he gently touched her arm. "Don't friends want to know everything about each other?"

His fingers caused the nerves in her arm to riot. She was sure he could see her heart thumping under her shirt, and she was afraid she was misunderstanding his meaning. "I had a best friend in boarding school. I'm not sure I'd want you to know what she knew."

He pulled back his hand. "Like . . ."

Without his hand touching her, she could think more clearly. "Like, I pretended to do badly in Spanish so a boy I liked at a neighboring school would coach me."

"And . . ."

"And I sent a birthday present to one of the Monkees."

"Monkeys?"

"The singing group. I idolized Davy Jones."

Nate chuckled. "Did he get it?"

"I don't know. But the fan club sent me a signed glossy picture that I taped on my mirror."

"These secrets aren't very deep or dark." Imps in his eyes teased her.

"Okay, you asked for it. You'll lose all respect for me when I tell you."

"Try me," he dared.

She looked around in mock fear to check if anyone else was listening. She whispered, "I used to pad my bra."

Nate threw back his head and laughed out loud—hearty laughter that filled the van.

Shara began laughing, too, and grabbed his elbow. "Stop that. It's embarrassing."

His laughter died down to a rueful grin. "Why do girls think they have to have—"

"Tell me that when you were a teenage boy, you didn't care." Her fingers were appreciating the strength of his muscles as she noticed how the short sleeves of his knit shirt hugged his upper arms.

"Oh, I looked. But there had to be more than breasts. The same is true now."

His voice almost caressed her. Shara shivered and released his arm. Her imagination was becoming overactive. She had gotten herself into this conversation and it was time she got out. "Okay, I told you some secrets, now tell me your weakness. Turnabout's fair play."

His heavy brows raised, his eyes sparkled, his chin tilted, and he looked positively rakish. "I'm a chocolate-ice-cream addict. Rocky road, double fudge, light chocolate, dark, soft or hard. And when I run out at home, I come here. I have to have it at least two or three times a week, or I'm grouchy and irritable."

Shara wondered how often Nate might be grouchy or irritable. When she worked with him and his employees on relaxation exercises, he had seemed to have an innate ability to shed his stress and relax no matter what method they used—biofeedback, breathing exercises, or self-hypnosis. She supposed that in his previous line of work, coping efficiently with extreme conditions was a must.

"Does Jerry know that chocolate will cure what ails you?" She teased.

"Jerry keeps chocolate Dixie Cups in the portable refrigerator in his office. But they don't always cure what ails me. Sometimes I need more than chocolate ice cream for that. Like a good listening ear or a hug. Jerry's not enthusiastic about hugs."

Again the undertone was there that he might want more than friendship. But she wasn't sure. "Hugs are important, maybe more important than food. I intend to give Danny so many hugs, he'll never be able to count them."

Nate's line of vision left her and moved over his shoulder to the sleeping child. He unbuckled his seat belt. "He looks like he's out for the night."

"He's been so restless the past few days. The heat's been miserable for him."

"And you." Nate opened his door. After walking around to Shara's side, he slid the side door open, crawled inside, and unbuckled the baby car seat. He picked up the seat with Danny still sleeping and took it to a picnic table set away from the others under a towering hickory tree.

When he bent over, his shorts hugged the firm curve of his buttocks. His movements were lithe and economical, indicating his superb physical condition. Shara opened her door, jumped out of the van, and followed him.

He gently set the seat on the wooden surface. "Chocolate or vanilla?"

"Do they have mixed?"

"You bet. I'll be right back."

Nate strode to the window at the ice-cream stand and ordered. While he waited, he looked over at Shara. He had taken a dangerous chance with some of his teasing. Although she'd backed away a bit, she hadn't closed him off. He wanted to spend time with her. To see what would happen. He had the feeling he was taking a step into territory much more dangerous than a war zone.

Taking the two cones back to the table, he sat down on the bench next to her. His knee brushed hers and she moved hers away. But she was close enough that he could smell the faint flowery scent of a soap or perfume. It tantalized him and made him want to move closer. Her low ponytail swept across her back in a silken wave as she tilted her head to lick her ice cream from the side. He'd love to release her hair from the tortoiseshell clasp and slide his fingers through it.

She gazed at him as if she was trying to work out a puzzle. He said simply, "You have beautiful hair. Have you always worn it long?"

Her hand went to her ponytail. "Since the Peace Corps. I went for two years without having it cut. It's cool in the summer, warms my neck in the winter, and it's versatile."

He imagined it spread out on a pillow—his pillow. He had to switch his thoughts to another track. "Why did you join the Peace Corps?"

She seemed to debate with herself before she answered. "I had my nursing degree and I didn't know what I wanted to do with it. I wanted independence, I wanted to be truly on my own. And I wanted to see how other people lived. The Peace Corps provided the vehicle for all that."

As the hot breeze slid across Nate's cheek, his elbow brushed Shara's arm companionably. The vibrations he felt were more than friendly. "A new life in a strange country, working with people who live differently than you do is damn hard. Did you have trouble adjusting?"

She took another lick of the soft ice cream, not keeping up with the drips along the cone. One landed on her palm.

Her tongue swept the sweetness from her hand. "At the beginning. Bolivia's a far cry from Pennsylvania. But people are people. Everyone has hopes and dreams. They want meaning in life whether that's raising healthy children, or farming, or learning to breed a new line of cattle. Some of the volunteers had the notion they were going to 'teach the natives.' That was the wrong idea."

Swatting at a bothersome fly that landed on Danny's arm, she added, "I had to become a native and work side by side to foster friendship and understanding or they never would have listened to me when I told them how to keep themselves and their children disease-free. I wasn't better than they were, I was different. We learned from each other."

Nate admired Shara. He had lived in foreign countries because he wanted the world to be smaller. He wanted to spread news so people could learn about each other, and through the truth, understand. Shara shared that goal. She was more than concerned, she was committed to making the world better.

As Shara's tongue twirled around the chocolate-and-vanilla ice cream, Nate forgot his own. She was so pretty, so sensual without knowing it.

Danny opened his eyes, yawned, and with a newborn's unfocused gaze, found Shara. She ran her finger across his chin. "Hi there! Did you get a good nap? It's much cooler out here." Danny flailed his arms joyfully and Shara smiled.

The evening shadows had given way to gray dusk and the moon wore a gold halo. Pinpricks of stars were making their appearance. Nate's eyes drifted back to Shara. He wished he'd brought his camera. Shara reminded him of moonbeams. She wasn't glaring like the sun's rays, not sharp like starshine, but mellow, glowing, almost holy.

Shara unexpectedly covered Nate's hand with hers. "Look. He's smiling, isn't he? Look at that expression!"

Her touch had an undeniable effect on Nate's body. He felt a surge of warmth and tried to pretend her affectionate gesture didn't affect him. "Of course he's smiling. Anybody who says it's gas doesn't know babies."

Shara's eyes swung up to his and said she was glad he understood. Her expression was so open he was swamped by the desire to close the few inches between them and kiss her. Slowly. For a long time. Instead, he lifted his napkin and gently wiped a sticky smudge above her lip. Communication passed between them, but he wasn't sure Shara knew its depth. He smiled and took a crunch out of his cone.

After they finished their ice cream, Nate drove Shara home. Danny was awake but quiet until they entered the town house. As sweltering heat rushed at them, Danny put his lungs to good use lodging a protest. Nate put the car seat on the sofa and Shara lifted Danny out. She rocked him in her arms but his cries became louder.

"I'm going upstairs to change him."

"Do you want me to warm a bottle? Or are you going to use the one you took along?"

She shook her head. "I'm afraid that was out too long. There are some in the refrigerator. Put it in the microwave for forty seconds." She started for the staircase and turned around. "Nate?"

"What?"

"Thanks."

He waved his hand as if she was being foolish and headed toward the kitchen.

Shara changed Danny, powdered him, tried to distract him, but nothing could quiet him. He was hungry, that's all, she told herself as perspiration dripped between her breasts. She put the back of her hand to her forehead. If she didn't get some sleep soon, she wouldn't do herself or Danny any good. Picking up her baby, she went downstairs.

Nate was ready for her. He took Danny from her arms and settled in the recliner as he had done earlier in the evening. But this time Danny was restless. He sucked for a minute, then turned his head away and wriggled in Nate's arms.

Shara watched as Nate patiently tried the bottle again and again and crooned softly. His deep baritone did funny things to her nervous system as if in some way she was connected to her son, and Nate was comforting her, too. What would it be like to be held in his strong arms, nurtured, touched? She remembered the night Jim died, the gentleness and tenderness of Nate's arms as he held her. She remembered the weight of his arm across her shoulders in the hospital, the casual touches she had assumed were merely friendly.

But tonight, every time their skin came into contact, the hairs on her neck stood up, her pulse raced, and she felt electrified. When she looked into his eyes, she felt as if she was hanging in midair. What was different between them? He was the same person. She was the same person. But now when they were together, they were different.

Her thoughts were shattered when Danny gave up all pretext of drinking and wailed. Nate shook his head helplessly and let Shara take the baby. She paced the room as she had for the last few days, hoping the crying would stop.

Abruptly, Nate stood up. "This is ridiculous, Shara. It's hot as blazes in here and probably worse upstairs. What are you going to do?"

"Pitch a tent in the yard?" she joked above the crying, trying to keep her sanity so she didn't start crying, too.

Nate dashed his hand through his black hair, disheveling it and making it stand on end. "Shara, go to a motel for few days. Get out of this heat so you can both be comfortable."

Didn't he know how farfetched his idea was? Didn't he realize the cost? That she could use the money for any number of better purposes? As she patted Danny's back and kissed the top of his head, she saw the look in Nate's eyes. Before the words came out, she knew what he was going to say.

"Let me pay for it, Shara." Before she could utter a protest, he used emotional persuasion. "You have to think of what's good for Danny. You can't be worried about your pride. Consider it a baby gift."

"Nate, it's not just pride." Shara rubbed her cheek against Danny's, hoping the loving contact would evaporate his discomfort. "It's feasibility, too. I need a refrigerator and stove. I'd need to take all his supplies. I wash and dry diapers every day. A motel room's not adequate. Besides, you've already given me too many gifts."

"So what are you going to do?" Frustration gathered around Nate's mouth and he looked fierce. "Go without sleep for another night? You're worn out, Shara. Be reasonable."

Danny wailed louder, emphasizing Nate's point.

Her expression must have still been set because Nate stepped closer and said, "There is another alternative."

She eyed him warily. "What?"

"Come stay with me for a few days."

FOUR

Shara's eyes became wider with astonishment. "You can't be serious!"

"I'm very serious. I have air conditioning and three bedrooms. There's plenty of room. I have a stove, a refrigerator, *and* a washer and dryer. Everything you need."

He looked as if he really meant his offer. "Nate, I can't."

"Because . . ." he drawled.

"Because I can't impose that way. You have your own life."

His tone was dry. "I promise you won't cramp my style. I don't have wild parties every night."

She wondered what he did do for entertainment, if he dated much and whom he dated. But it wasn't any of her business. Danny's crying went up a decibel. "Listen to this. Are you willing to have a baby around?"

Nate took Danny from Shara, held the baby in the tender crook of his arm, and rocked him. Danny's crying subsided to a whimper. "Once you get out of this heat, he'll feel better, you'll feel better. Trust me."

Trust him. Trust a man to help give her what she needed. No, he wasn't saying that. He was offering her a cooler place to stay. It might help. But . . .

"There might be talk, Nate. You're well known in this community."

"So are you. I don't see a problem. I'm helping a friend. There's nothing wrong with that. Besides, I'm in a secluded area. No one will know you're there."

"I have to tell Amber."

Nate waited silently for Shara to make a decision.

Danny's whimper began to gain force. She rubbed her forefinger against her temple and closed her eyes. After a moment she opened them. "Okay. But there's so much to take—the bassinet, the bottles, the diaper pail."

"The van has plenty of room."

He was meeting every one of her objections with logic and practicality. She was a practical person. She smiled. "Let's get out of this heat."

Shara had never been to Nate's house. They drove past the hospital and York College, turning up into the hills away from the city. She couldn't make out the structure of the houses they passed; many of them were hidden by trees. Shara saw light glimmering through giant elms before she saw Nate's house. The porch light was burning brightly, as well as a light above the garage. When Nate pulled into the driveway, she looked at the compact contemporary home with interest. The exterior was clad in vertical cedar planks and the roof had a distinctive design with an overhang sheltering clerestory windows.

"Is this solar?" she asked curiously.

"It's called a passive solar home. There's a solarium in the back that collects the sun's heat during daylight. There are thermal floors there and in the living room. When the sun sets, they release heat to the other areas. The insulation helps keep the house cool in summer, but in this heat, I've been using the back-up system."

As Shara held Danny in her arms and walked through the house looking around, Nate brought in everything she needed to make Danny comfortable. The central foyer led to a generously proportioned living room. It was made dramatic by a sloped ceiling and an immense stone fireplace. Her sandals clicked on the ceramic tiles as she walked through the living room to peek into the solarium that opened onto a backyard garden terrace.

Tracing her steps back to the foyer, she walked into the U-shaped kitchen. It had an unusual corner sink and every modern appliance imaginable. There was a dinette area on one side of the kitchen, a formal dining room on the other. The dining room opened into the living room, forming a large, continuous space.

Shara loved the roominess and friendliness of the house. Nate had furnished it in dark pine, the main colors being navy and peach tones. The extra-long sofa could accommodate his length. The squat, puffy-cushioned chairs invited lounging. There were no draperies anywhere but instead slim, slatted cream-colored blinds that could let in an overabundance of sunshine or shut it out entirely.

Nate called down from the balcony of the loft that overlooked the living room. "I can put the bassinet in here. I'll clean off the desk and you can use it as a changing table."

"Nate, I don't want to disrupt your office."

"You won't be a disruption, Shara."

The certainty in Nate's voice assured Shara he wanted her in his home. "I think you'd better put him in with me for tonight. I don't want him to be frightened."

Nate nodded, and a few seconds later Shara heard his footfalls coming down the steps. He came into the living room and grinned when he saw Danny peacefully sucking on his fist. "See? I knew he'd like it here."

Shara brushed Danny's fine hair over his forehead. "The air-conditioning feels lovely."

"Glad you came?"

Nate's eyes seemed to invite her into more than his home, but she answered honestly. "Yes."

He waved to the kitchen. "My microwave works the same as yours if you want to try another bottle and get Danny settled. I already put them in the refrigerator."

Shara warmed a bottle and took Danny upstairs. Nate had laid her suitcase on the bed. Shara changed Danny and was feeding him in the bedside chair when Nate came into the room with two glasses of lemonade. Sweat was gleaming on his forehead from the exertion of carrying supplies from the van and his knit shirt molded to his chest.

He wiped his wrist across his brow, placed Shara's lemonade on a magazine on the night stand, and plunked down on the bed. "How's he doing?"

She dragged her eyes from Nate's chest. "Fine. Almost finished." She wiggled the bottle in Danny's mouth. "He's sleeping." Transferring the baby to her shoulder, she patted his back until he burped. She stood up and laid him in the bassinet on his stomach.

Nate drank the last of his lemonade. "If you'd like to take a shower, feel free."

Shara opened her suitcase. "That sounds great. I feel so sticky."

"You don't look sticky."

When she raised her gaze, his eyes caught hers. She was tongue-tied and didn't know what to say or do. As Nate stood up, his nose was only a few inches away from hers. She could feel the heat radiating from his body as she became lost in his eyes. There was a pull, such a pull, for her to reach up and stroke his face. He smelled of a discreet cologne and exertion, a male scent that was heady and almost made her dizzy. Nate stooped toward her slowly and placed a fleeting kiss on her cheek. So fleeting she wondered if she imagined it.

He straightened. "I'm going to do some work in my office. Just call in when you're finished in the bathroom. Don't hurry on my account. I'll probably be working for a while." He brushed where his lips had touched with his forefinger and left the room.

Nate walked briskly to the loft and sat down heavily in the swivel chair. It groaned with his weight and he stretched out his legs under the desk. This was a damn stupid decision inviting Shara to stay with him. He felt like he was sinking in quicksand. But what else could he do? It was the logical and chivalrous thing to do. Hah! Chivalrous. He'd have to remember that when he couldn't sleep tonight. Every time he got within two feet of her, he wanted to take her in his arms . . .

Put it out of your head, McKendrick. Way out.

He pulled a sheaf of papers from the right side of the desk to the blotter and read them in earnest. He was making notes in the margin in red ink when Shara appeared in the doorway. She wore a pale yellow gown and robe, her hair flowing full and free around her face with a just-dried glossiness. He smelled the fragile scent of flowers and felt a tense tightening in the pit of his stomach. When she smiled at him, his breath caught in his chest.

"I'm finished in the bathroom and I'm going to bed. I don't know how long I'll have until Danny wakes up, and I want to take advantage of it."

Nate cleared his throat. "Sure, you go right ahead. I keep strange hours."

Shara's eyes landed on Nate's foot. He was tapping it nervously. "I hope I won't disturb you when I get up in the middle of the night."

He planted his feet firmly on the floor and lifted his shoulders. "Don't worry about it."

Shara watched his fingers toy with a letter opener. The back of his hand was sprinkled with fine black hair. His long fingers looked so manly. Her skin began to tingle as her mind began to imagine those hands . . . She looked away from his fingers back to his face, startled by her reaction to her thoughts. "Well, I'll say good night then. I'll see you sometime tomorrow."

"Right." He seemed to be waiting for her to leave. Shara smiled shyly and went back to her room. She closed the door so Nate wouldn't hear Danny when he cried. While she turned down the green flowered quilt and stark-white sheet, she couldn't understand her mixed emotions. Something was happening between her and Nate. Something powerful. It scared her. She gazed at her sleeping son, took comfort from his peaceful sleep, and turned off the light.

A light sleeper, Nate awakened when he heard footsteps going down the staircase. He had worked until two A.M., trying to forget Shara was twenty feet away. A cold shower had only made him wish she was in the shower with him, or the whirlpool tub, or in his bed . . . Damn!

He was almost out the bedroom door before he realized he was naked. Snatching a pair of worn flannel jogging shorts from his chair, he stepped into them and went downstairs. He hadn't heard Danny crying and he presumed Shara had the baby downstairs with her.

But he found her alone, washing out a bottle. "Is everything all right?"

She turned away from the sink. "He's asleep. I already gave him his . . ." She stopped when she saw Nate's bare chest. Wavy black hair wisped around his bronze nipples. The line of hair arrowed down the middle of his chest and disappeared under the elastic waistband of his shorts. From the way they clung, she knew he wore nothing underneath.

His body was everything she could imagine a man's body should be. Hard, muscled, taut. Her heart began beating fast, faster, as her cheeks grew hot. She set the bottle down on the counter before she dropped it. Had Danny's birth released a new batch of hormones that gave her X-rated thoughts? This was Nate, for Pete's sake. A friend. But a small voice whispered, *There's more than a friendly look in his eyes*.

Nate's nostrils twitched and she guessed he smelled the lotion she had smoothed all over her body. His hand came up and stopped in midair. "Shara . . ."

Nate was looking at her with a pained expression on his face. She wondered why until she belatedly realized the glow from the light over the sink outlined her body under the sheer cotton nightgown. She hadn't bothered with a robe because she thought she'd be alone.

She stepped back against the corner cabinet. "I'm sorry if I woke you."

His voice was husky. "I thought you might need something."

As he walked slowly toward her, her heart beat frantically. With each step he took, something inside her woke up, came more alive than she'd ever felt it. "I'm capable, Nate. I'm capable of taking care of myself and Danny."

"I've never doubted that. I just thought I might be able to help." If he was smart, he'd make an excuse and get back to his bedroom fast. But he couldn't be smart. Not when she looked like an angel standing in front of him, not when she smelled like a summer garden, not when he wanted to hold her and touch her everywhere more than he wanted to breathe.

Shara took a step closer to him. "I don't know if I'm ready for help."

His hands came up of their own accord and grasped her shoulders. "Anybody's help, or my help?"

She searched his face, aware of her breasts only inches from his chest. She felt them peak and realized her body was asking for closer contact. She wanted his lips on hers. She wanted to feel like a woman again. Not just with anybody, but with Nate. He was strong yet gentle, intelligent and kind. She trembled from the strength of her need.

"What are you afraid of, Shara?" His thumbs caressed her collarbone.

His touch made her drunk and she reflexively swayed closer. "I have a child to think about and . . . I don't want to get hurt."

Neither did he. But right now the present held more fascination than anything that might happen in the future. His hands moved up her neck, under her hair. He splayed them and let her hair flow through the spaces. "So soft. I've never seen hair as shiny and soft and long." Releasing her hair, he ran his fingertips from her shoulders to her elbows. "Your skin's so white, so silky. I've wanted to touch it for a very long time."

She was overwhelmed by the velvet depth of his voice, the silver light in his eyes, the penetrating tenderness of his touch. Her hands went to his shoulders and as her fingers curled, her sigh was captured by his firm, warm lips. They were a sensual delight. They quested slowly, awakening dormant desire. His tongue slipped along the seam of her lips until she opened to him. He invaded slowly, filling her, completing her in some way. When he began stroking, kaleidoscopic colors bathed her in warmth. The oranges and reds embraced, became a fiery ball in her womb, and spread until the blues and purples and greens disappeared and the crimson invaded every nerve.

Nate's arms tightened until she was pressed close enough to feel the thrust of his arousal. When she moved against him, he groaned, and she realized her power. She could feel muscle and sinew and strength—so much strength.

With the reverence of first discovery, Nate's hands stroked up and down Shara's back. He wanted to be rid of the frustrating material but couldn't think straight enough to figure out how. His large hands progressed lower to cup her bottom. He had wanted to touch her, hold her, for so long. He brought her tighter against his hips. But that was a mistake. She was too soft; he was too hard. Fireworks exploded.

An alarm went off in his head. He tried to ignore it. It sounded again and he had to ask, did she want this? If she didn't, if she was only participating because she was vulnerable . . . Damn! He felt like a plane that had over-shot its runway and landed on its nose instead of its wheels.

Nate's hands stilled. He swore again to himself as he released her, blaming himself for letting this happen too soon. What if she hated him for this? What if she ran out of his life? His eyes were turbulent as he stepped back and dropped his arms to his sides.

Shara opened her eyes and saw his expression. He looked as if the IRS had called him in for an audit. "Nate, it's all right," she said hoarsely. "I wanted that as much as you did."

The air whooshed from his lungs in relief. "Lord, I'm glad you said that."

"What did you think I'd do? Slap you? That's a bit melodramatic." A telltale flush of passion stained her cheeks.

"I'm not worried about a slap."

"What are you worried about?"

"I'm worried I've ruined our . . . friendship, worried you'll deny the chemistry between us."

There was too much to absorb—the change in their rela-tionship, her own desire that seemed to spring up from nowhere, conflicting feelings she had to sort out. "Nate, I'd better not stay here. Tomorrow morning I'll go back to my apartment."

This was exactly what he'd been afraid of. He might not know how involved he should get, but he knew he didn't want her to leave. He needed to buy some time. "It's late. You need your sleep, Danny needs his. Promise me you'll stay until after supper tomorrow night. Just see how things go." The longer Shara stayed, the better were his chances of persuading her to stay even longer.

Looking shaky and pensive, she seemed to be deciding whether running was safer than staying. She crossed her arms over her breasts as if she could hide the intimacy they had shared. "I'll stay until tomorrow evening."

Nate wanted to hold her, to somehow prove to her everything would be all right, but she looked closed, defensive, lost in thought. There was nothing more he could say or do now. He reached out and touched a strand of her hair. "Go up to bed. And when you're thinking, think about the kiss."

Shara passed by Nate, and after a last look, mounted the stairs.

Much later Shara heard Danny crying in the far recesses of her mind. But she couldn't swim out of the fog. She felt a hand on her shoulder. "Go back to sleep. I'll feed him."

"Nate," she said groggily.

"Go back to sleep."

Slumberland definitely held more allure than warming a bottle. She mumbled good night, closed her eyes, and fell back to sleep.

When Shara awoke again, bright sunlight was streaking the bedroom. She yawned, stretched, and wondered what was wrong. She looked over at the bassinet. It was gone. For a moment she panicked, but then she remembered Nate. After she put on her robe, she heard a low voice coming from Nate's office. She walked down the hall and peeked in. Danny was propped in his car seat on a chair next to the desk. Nate was turned away from the scribbling on the legal pad on his desk and was shaking a rattle and trying to get Danny to follow it with his eyes.

She couldn't suppress a smile. "You're getting a lot of work done."

Nate swiveled around. "Do you know what a genius you have here? He can follow this with his eyes already."

When Shara's gaze met Nate's, there was spontaneous combustion. She moved toward her son, away from Nate. "I think that has more to do with the senses than intelligence."

Nate looked as if his senses were on the alert. He seemed to be enjoying her just-awakened blush and ruffled appearance. "Nonsense. He'll be reading at age four."

To take her mind off the sensations vibrating between them, she asked, "How did you get so good with babies? Most men think they'll break. But you aren't afraid to pick him up or hold him."

The chair squeaked when Nate leaned back. "I told you Brad was born at home."

Shara nodded her head in acknowledgement.

Crossing his ankle over his knee, Nate looked relaxed. "Mom's delivery wasn't as easy as yours. She needed help the first few weeks and, like you said, Dad was afraid Brad would break. I was ten and took Brad on as my personal responsibility. Brad was five when our father left for greener pastures. I became his father figure."

"That must have been difficult for you."

"It was. I lost my childhood."

"I never knew my biological father," Shara said tentatively. "He wouldn't marry my mother because he wanted to finish college."

"How did she manage?"

"She'd been a secretary for an insurance agency during summers. She dropped out of college and worked there full time before and after I was born."

"You mentioned a stepfather." Nate's voice was interested and caring, not prying.

"She married one of the clients of the agency—a very well-to-do client."

"You aren't happy about that?"

She never talked about her childhood indiscriminately. But she felt the need to tell Nate. "My stepfather thinks of my mom as a decoration. He always has. Climbing to the top rung of the social ladder is his aim in life. My mother helps him do that. She's attractive, intelligent, and never contradicts him."

"Did you and he get along?"

"Not particularly." It still hurt to think about. He'd always kept himself removed, and she'd felt like a responsibility he pawned off on to others. "How did your mom cope?"

"After Dad left, she was a real trooper. Eventually she went back to school and earned a degree in business management. She's an account manager in a publishing company. They print mostly medical journals."

"Is that how you got interested in journalism?"

"I snooped around the presses and the art and stripping departments. But I had a teacher in high school who got me interested in photography. My senior year I did a special layout on our track and field day and wrote the copy to go with it. It won an award from the Chamber of Commerce and that got me started. I knew the direction I was headed and what I wanted to do. How about you? How did you get involved in health promotion?"

"The Peace Corps helped me decide. When I was in Bolivia, I discovered I didn't want to help people *after* they became sick. I wanted to help prevent them from *getting* sick. So when I returned, I went to Johns Hopkins for my master's in public health. It's a wonderful and growing field. I love working in it." She looked over at the cooing baby. "But I love taking care of him more. That's why I want to stay home as long as I can."

Keeping his eyes on Shara's face was difficult for Nate with her standing there in her robe with the little yellow bow he'd love to untie. Just thinking about kissing her was enough to get his hormones churning. It was time to be practical. "Are you ready for breakfast?"

She looked at the digital clock on his desk. "More like brunch. I hope you didn't wait for me to eat."

He stood up and picked up Danny's car seat. "I went for a jog and had something to eat after Danny went back to sleep at seven."

"Nate, you didn't have to do that. I could have gotten up—"

"I wanted to do it. Consider this a vacation. Besides, you know you needed the sleep."

"Nate, I still think I should leave."

He took Danny into the hall. "We'll talk about it after brunch."

Shara did her sit-ups, brushed her teeth, dressed in a pink cotton blouse and culottes, and took a deep breath to relax. She'd never been fainthearted about facing life. But she wasn't sure what Nate was suggesting. There was a definite chemistry between them. Last night's kiss proved that. But she didn't know what he wanted. She didn't know what *she* wanted. When Nate was near, her senses kicked into overdrive and rational thinking became difficult.

She thought about Jim. She'd never reacted this strongly to his scent, his texture, his touch. Probably because he was more intent on satisfying his needs rather than hers. She met him when they were giving lectures on career day at a high school. She'd needed someone to love and someone who would love her back. His boyish appeal had wrapped itself around her heart. She had seen him as a hero, saving other people's lives. She hadn't realized until too late that he didn't have the time to put that same energy into their marriage. She'd thought marriage would bring a new depth to their relationship. He didn't want depth. He liked making love, he liked sharing her company, but he hadn't wanted the responsibility of working on communication or finances, or the spiritual side of loving that was so important to Shara.

And Nate?

Nate. The smell of frying bacon wafted up the stairs. She had to make a decision. He was treating her so tenderly, so gently. Tears pricked in her eyes. It had been so long since someone cared for her. She lifted her brush from the dresser and brushed her hair until it gleamed. Then she went downstairs.

Nate looked her over with male approval. The circles weren't so dark under her eyes and she looked rested. She also looked . . . worried. "Hungry?"

She tickled Danny's foot. He was lying in his car seat in the middle of the table. "Starved."

Nate grinned. "Good. Pop some bread in the toaster, will you?"

"Nate, you don't have to wait on me. I could have fixed my own breakfast."

"It's as easy to do for two as one."

"You already ate."

"Consider it my midmorning snack."

Shara laughed and eyed his long body. "I'll bet you're expensive to feed."

"That's what Mom always claimed, but I never

believed her until I started buying my own food and cooking for myself.''

Shara removed the twistie from the plastic bag and put two slices of bread in the toaster. ''After brunch I'm going to launder the diapers and sterilize the bottles.''

Nate took the bacon from the frying pan and laid it on a paper towel on a plate so it drained. He faced Shara squarely. ''And after that?'' He saw Shara's uncertainty. ''The heat wave's not going to break until the end of the week.''

Shara opened the refrigerator and found the butter in the door. She set it on the table. ''I don't know if I feel comfortable staying.''

''Because of what happened last night?''

''That's part of it. And because I'm having feelings I'm not sure what to do with.''

''About me?''

She nodded.

His grin was lopsided and pleased. ''I'm glad about that.''

''Oh, Nate,'' she sighed and sat down in a chair at the table.

''What if I promise you last night won't happen again? Not unless you want it to.''

She moved the salt shaker back and forth a few inches with her long hair hiding her face. ''What I want and what I think I should do are two different things. I don't think either of us should make a promise we can't or don't want to keep.''

''I keep my promises, Shara.''

The strength of his voice brought her head up. ''Even if you do, if we deny what we're feeling, we'll be walking on eggs.''

He switched off the gas burner under the eggs, crossed to her, and took her chin in his hand. "What if I promise that even if last night happens again, I won't let it get out of hand."

"Can you really promise that?"

"Of course I can. Shara, you just had a baby. I'm not going to let anything happen that shouldn't. Not until you're ready."

"What do you want from me, Nate?"

His expression said she'd taken him off guard; his cheeks flushed. "I'm not sure."

She cut straight to the heart, her eyes combing his steadily. "Sex?"

He bristled. "I'm not just looking for a body to warm my bed."

"Nate, I have to think about Danny."

His face gentled. "I know. I guess I want some time. I live from day to day, not usually thinking about the future."

"I can't do that," she said softly. While living with Jim, anxiety had become a way of life. His job and his attitude put more pressure on her than she wanted to handle. She'd coped by organizing and planning.

"Have you ever tried it?"

"In Bolivia."

"And what happened?" His gray eyes demanded the truth.

"Life fell into place."

He grinned. "Care to try it again?"

"I don't know if I can. A lot's happened. When I was married to Jim—"

He stroked her cheek with the back of his hand. "Tell me."

She let her lashes flutter down so he couldn't see the hunger his touch provoked. "I had to be the responsible one, pay the bills, get the cars inspected. He was too busy fighting fires. I had to plan because he didn't."

Nate lifted her chin with his knuckle. "I'm not talking about being irresponsible. I'm talking about grabbing each moment and living it to the fullest."

It would be wonderful to live that way again. Especially with Nate. "I could try. But, Nate . . . I'm not rushing into anything."

He took her face between his palms. "I know. And I won't push you. Will you stay until your air-conditioning is fixed?" His faint smile was coaxing and it made her smile, too.

Ushering up a silent prayer that she was doing the right thing, she answered, "I'll stay. But only if you let me pull my weight. You can help with Danny if you let me cook suppers and if you promise to tell me when we get in your way."

At that moment Danny chose to make his presence known. He began crying and waving his hands.

Nate shrugged and said matter-of-factly, "He's hungry, too."

When Shara rose, she stood nose-to-nose with Nate. She moved to the right. He moved to the same side. He moved to the left. She moved to the left. They both began laughing. Nate dropped his arm around her shoulders and said close to her ear, "Sometime we'll try genuine dancing and see how we match up."

Shara's stomach coiled tightly at the thought and Nate's nearness. Dancing with him would be an unforgettable experience. But if he held her now, the embrace would be more than friendly. Staying here with him might be a mistake. Leaving could be an even bigger one.

FIVE

Nate sat on the sofa, listening to the soft strains of an easy-listening radio station flowing from the speakers. Shara was phoning Amber to tell her friend her plans. Danny was sleeping, having been bathed and fed before Shara's call. It felt odd having other people in the house, a woman and a baby in the house. The atmosphere unsettled Nate and pleased him at the same time.

When Shara walked into the room, he put down the magazine he held and patted the cushion next to him on the sofa. She sat down with a cautious smile. Did she think he was going to jump her? In a way, he guessed he was.

Nate stretched his arm along the back of the sofa. "I'd like to ask you something."

"Sure."

"Why were you and Jim getting a divorce?"

Shara was silent as she dropped her eyes to her lap. "No matter what I did, what I gave, it wasn't enough," she finally said. "I couldn't compete with his love of firefighting. His career was a vocation and it came first. He went to fires when he wasn't even on duty. His job came before sharing with me, it came before our financial well-being, it came before logic and common sense."

Nate lowered his arm to her shoulders. It was obvious she was still trying to figure out what she could have done differently, or better. "He was a fool, Shara. You're not a woman to take for granted."

She was stiff and tense. "I kept asking myself what was wrong with me? Why wasn't I enough? What more could I have done?"

"What more *could* you have done?" Maybe he could give her some perspective.

She angled her body away from him and braced her shoulder against the sofa. "I don't know. Maybe if I had gotten pregnant early in our marriage . . ."

Nate lifted her chin and said with decisiveness, "A child might not have made a difference."

"Intellectually I know that." She paused and looked at the wall behind him. "Sometimes I wonder if he was reckless that night on purpose. He didn't want the divorce. If he was depressed and it was my fault—"

He knew the hunger that had driven Jim. It had nothing to do with Shara and he had to make her see that. "Don't carry a burden that isn't yours. He died because he made a poor judgment. He went in too far without his mask. His death was his own fault—not yours."

"I saw a friend who's a therapist after Jim died. That's what she tried to make me see."

Nate saw the cloud cover lift in her eyes, as if she could finally believe Jim controlled his own destiny. "If you need to talk about Jim or your feelings, don't hesitate. I'm here for you."

When he stroked her face, she covered his hand with hers and sat back against the sofa. As she slackened against him, her muscles relaxed. His stiffened. Not from tension but from desire. She shifted and her breast grazed his chest. He almost groaned from the ache to hold her closer, to feel her body against his. But he couldn't act on his impulses. She trusted him; he wouldn't betray that trust.

When a Top-Forty ballad flowed from the stereo, Nate suggested, "Let's dance."

"Here?"

He was enthusiastic. "Sure, here." Cocking his head, he kidded, "Of course, maybe you'd prefer the Rainbow Room. I could make reservations two weeks from next Saturday."

She laughed. A sweet, free sound that blended with the music. "A dance at the Rainbow Room could cost you a week's salary."

Dinner and dancing at one of New York City's finest restaurants wasn't an everyday occurrence for the average woman. But Shara wasn't the average woman. "You'd be worth it," Nate quipped as he stood up and pulled her up next to him.

They were both in their bare feet, and Shara felt silly when Nate guided her to the center of the tiled living room away from the edge of the Oriental carpet. He put his arm around her, letting his hand rest in the small of her back. He took her right hand and held it in the standard ballroom position. They made the traditional box with Nate guiding Shara into a few adaptations.

"You're good."

He leaned back and grinned. "Don't sound so surprised! I *have* learned a few social graces."

She couldn't prevent her fingers from softly kneading his shoulder. His knit shirt couldn't hide his strength. Nate brought her hand into his chest and pulled her a little closer. He was holding her loosely enough that she could pull back if she wanted to. She didn't want to. Her head fit nicely into the groove of his shoulder. Nate's chin brushed against her temple. He rubbed it against her hair as if the action gave him a great deal of pleasure.

She was feeling pleasure herself. She had thawed into him and his thighs were guiding their movement. His hair-roughened legs were erotic against her smooth ones. Their steps became fewer, and a gentle sway felt like dancing on a cloud. Her breasts pushed against his chest, and when he moved, her nipples stood up with the friction. Pleasure became an insidious heat that began at her breasts, made a connection in her womb, and spread to her fingertips and toes.

When Nate's hand abandoned hers, she wrapped her arms around his neck. Their eyes locked. Nate's hands stroked up and down her back, bringing her closer, closer. They stopped moving. Shara's hands slid into the thickness of his black hair. He touched his lips to her forehead, the corner of her mouth, her chin, and began a trail down the length of her neck. When he came to the V of her blouse, he stopped and she almost cried out in frustration. She had never been kissed and held like this—so tenderly, so sensually.

She bent her head back and said, "Kiss me, Nate. Please kiss me."

The silver light in his eyes said he was delighted to oblige. She couldn't tell if it was her heart making all that racket or his. She only knew that when his lips found hers, she felt honored, cherished. He was so gentle. Her tongue came out to play and the tip touched the inside of his lip. His reaction was instantaneous. He was aroused, becoming harder. His tongue forgot to be gentle and went on a search mission to discover all her secrets. His hands kneaded her roundness and pushed her up and into him.

Ricocheting stars sprinkled her with their light and heat until she moaned into his mouth and attempted to give more. What would his hands feel like on her breasts? What would his body feel like on top of hers? He would be a gentle lover, a persuasive lover . . . Lord, a lover! *What* was she thinking about? She doubted if she was physically ready. She hadn't asked the doctor because she didn't think it would be an issue. It *was* an issue because she was seriously considering . . .

Nate backed off before she did. He let his lips cling so she knew he didn't want to pull away. Supporting her until her feet were flat on the floor, he said, "I promised I wouldn't let anything get out of hand. It almost did. Shara, when I kiss you . . ." There was longing in his eyes.

Shara took her hands from around his neck. "We might have to keep the kisses shorter." She smiled shakily. "I almost got lost and couldn't find my way back."

Nate locked his hands at her back waist. "I'll help you find your way and we'll get an egg timer for the kisses."

Her smile bloomed into laughter. "And who's going to watch the timer?"

"Danny, of course." Nate's wink was pure Casanova.

Shara poked him in the ribs so he'd release her and she repeated wryly, "Of course."

* * *

Two weeks later on a Sunday afternoon, Shara fluttered around her kitchen nervously, making sure she had two of Danny's pacifiers sterilized and enough bottles in the refrigerator to take care of an afternoon and evening. Amber was sitting at the bright-yellow table for two, paging through a woman's magazine.

Shara looked in the refrigerator again and then closed the door. "If you need more formula, the cans are in the cupboard."

"Shara, will you relax? I can take care of everything Danny needs. Just go to the baseball game and have fun."

When Nate had asked Shara to go with him to an Orioles game, she automatically said yes. But then she realized she needed a baby-sitter. She knew she could trust Amber, but she was anxious about leaving Danny for the first time. Since her stay at Nate's house, Nate had visited her often. She'd made supper and they'd spent the evenings talking, going for long drives, exploring parts of York even she hadn't seen. Nate's camera was always beside him ready for a new scene, a different picture. Danny was with them and Nate seemed to like it that way. He was excellent with Danny. But today it would be the two of them—alone.

"Shara, what are you thinking about?" Amber asked.

"This is the first time I'll be leaving Danny. The first time Nate and I will be . . . out in public."

"So what's the big deal? The stadium has pay phones. You can call every half hour if you must. And as far as Nate goes, it's about time you went out in public with a man. You don't have to hide or answer to anybody but yourself."

Amber was never tactful when she made a point, and

Shara had known her too long to take offense. She said quietly, ''I have to get used to being with a man again.''

''Seems to me it wouldn't be hard to get used to if he's the right man. I'm going to say something, and when I do, don't hit the ceiling. A father for your son would be nice. A husband for you wouldn't be bad, either. And don't give me that glare. You're the marrying type and you need a man who appreciates you. Jim didn't. It sounds like Nate does.''

Shara almost wished she hadn't been quite so candid with Amber about her marriage to Jim. But she had needed someone to talk to during the separation, and Amber had been willing to listen.

''How do you know if it's the right man? Is Leon the right man for you?''

''I'm not sure I'm marrying material, and don't change the subject. You'll know if Nate's right—in your heart. You didn't wait for that with Jim. You assumed he wanted the same things you did. He didn't. He couldn't. His patron saint was Peter Pan.''

Shara felt she had to defend him, though she didn't know why. ''He saved lives.''

''Yeah. And he didn't care about yours. He wasn't even responsible enough to take out a decent life insurance policy.''

''I didn't feel right accepting what he did have.''

''You deserved it. His child deserved it.''

To get Amber away from the subject, Shara sat down across from her. ''I'll have extra money coming in for next Saturday. Someone at work mistakenly scheduled two seminars for the same morning. I hate to ask you to baby-sit again—''

Amber wrinkled her nose. ''I would. But I can't. Leon

and I are going to his mother's for the weekend.'' She snapped her fingers. ''But I know someone who probably can. The secretary at work uses her all the time. I'll ask about her.''

''It has to be someone dependable, who I can meet and talk to ahead of time.''

''Of course. And don't ever hesitate to ask me to baby-sit. Maybe it's because I know my biological clock's ticking, but I really enjoy it.''

The doorbell rang before Shara could comment. Amber gave her a wink with the thumbs-up sign and followed her into the living room. When Shara opened the screen door, her heart skipped a few beats. True to his word, Nate was keeping their kisses short, but they were still potent enough to rattle the straps on her sandals. Whenever she saw him, it was almost reflexive to want to dive into his arms. But she smiled instead and introduced him to Amber. When Nate turned away to look at Danny in his bassinet, Amber's grin spread from one ear to the other and she rolled her eyes in approval.

After Shara and Nate were settled in the van, he leaned over and took her hand. ''I'd like to kiss you, but you're too far away, and even if I could, I have a feeling Amber would watch us from the window.''

Shara laughed, then said, ''She probably would. She was giving me a lecture when you arrived.''

''About?''

''Getting on with my life.''

''She sounds like a good friend.'' His index finger brushed gently over the life line on her palm.

Shara was distracted by the pressure of his finger, the sensuality of his touch. ''Oh, great. I'd better not leave the two of you alone in the same room. You'll gang up on me."

His finger moved to the pulse point on her wrist. "The only woman I want to be in a room alone with is you."

"We're alone today." She knew he could feel the increase in her pulse rate.

"Yes, we are, and we're going to take advantage of every minute." He placed a soft kiss on the center of her palm, faced the steering wheel, and switched on the ignition.

They talked and laughed on the drive to Baltimore, enjoying each other's company. When they arrived at Memorial Stadium, Nate pulled out a parking pass. Since the park was in the middle of the city, parking could be a problem. Without a pass, they would have had to park in a different lot, bumper to bumper, unable to leave until the game was over and the fans dispersed.

Nate led Shara to box seats under cover from the afternoon sun. When Shara looked down, third base was right in front of her. "Who do you know to get seats like this?"

He winked. "I have connections."

Shara liked baseball games—the open air, the excitement of live action, the array of spectators. After the fourth inning, Nate laid his hand on Shara's knee. Her blood heated from his touch and she looked away from the melee on the field to him.

"Would you like to get something to eat?" he asked. "I want to take you someplace nice for dinner after the game but that could be a while. While we're down there, you could call Amber."

Sometimes the man was downright clairvoyant. "I'd like to call Amber. If you know where we're going for dinner, I could give her the name of the restaurant. Just in case."

He laid the baseball program under his seat, took off his sunglasses and hung them on the pocket of his T-shirt, all the while still holding her knee. "I developed some pictures of Danny I want you to see. We could stop and get them and you can call her again before we go to dinner."

Shara covered Nate's large hand with her smaller one, thankful he understood her concern for Danny. Another man might have been jealous or piqued because her mind wasn't totally on him.

Nate and Shara shared a plate of nachos and dip. Their eyes connected, their fingers brushed, and Shara realized she was falling in love.

After the trip back to York, Nate drove to his house. He headed to the darkroom in the basement while Shara went to the kitchen for a glass of water. The light on Nate's answering machine was blinking. When Nate brought the photos upstairs and spread them out on the dinette table, Shara smiled with delight. He had caught twelve expressions of Danny, each unique.

"These are wonderful!" When she looked up, she saw her praise meant a lot to him.

He studied the pictures over her shoulder. "I can't miss with Danny. He has so much personality. Did you call Amber?"

Engrossed in the likenesses of her son, she waved at the phone. "No, but you have a message."

Nate crossed to the machine, rewound the tape, and played it back. Shara heard, "McKendrick. It's Mason. I have something for you. Call me back ASAP."

Shara wondered who Mason was as Nate dialed a number without referring to the Rolodex on the counter. She listened to Nate's side of the conversation while she picked out her favorite picture.

Nate's voice was sharp and businesslike. "When did it happen? You want me there tonight? Sure, I understand. I thought they stopped transporting that by train. Do I need anything besides the photographic equipment? Right. Who should I contact when I get there? He knows I'm coming? Okay. I'll call you when I'm finished. You want a layout on the clean-up, too? Sure. I'll talk to you soon."

As soon as Nate hung up, he made another call and secured a plane reservation for midnight. When he was finished, he came over to stand beside Shara. She looked at him with speculative green eyes.

"I have to go to Pittsburgh for a few days."

The conversation hadn't sounded like a family emergency. It sounded as if Nate was working for someone. Who? Why? She asked a more practical question. "You're leaving tonight?"

"Yes. But we can still have dinner. There's plenty of time before my plane leaves."

Interest in Danny's pictures forgotten, she asked, "What are you going to do? I mean why are you going to Pittsburgh?"

"There's been a train wreck and a chemical spill. The officials are worried the bromine could get into the water supply. I'm not sure of the details yet. Mason wants me to get all the photographs I can get before the EPA starts clean-up operations."

"Who's Mason?"

"Charles Mason. He's the editor of the US Review."

Shara was confused. The national magazine Nate was talking about was top-notch, elite in its field. It included photo spreads with most of its stories. But what did Nate have to do with it? "So why did Mason call you and why are you going? I don't understand."

The look in his eyes was pure astonishment. "I thought you knew. I do assignments like this whenever they call me. It keeps me in the field."

"How long are you usually gone?" Her monotone was in direct defiance of what she was feeling.

"That depends. Usually no more than a week."

Her voice was a whisper. "How many weeks out of the year?"

"One or two a month, sometimes less."

"That often?" She couldn't believe this. She couldn't believe Nate spent so much time away. She couldn't believe she was falling for another man who wouldn't make her a top priority. And what about Danny? He needed stability, a consistent role model. Not someone who came and went on a whim.

When he moved toward her, she backed away. "Why didn't you tell me you still roamed all over God's creation? I thought your past was behind you. I thought you owned a newspaper and you'd settled down. But you haven't!"

"I thought you knew. Everybody does. Jerry, the reporters, even the secretaries. When you were working with the staff at the *Herald*, I went out of town for a few days. Don't you remember?"

"I thought that had something to do with running the paper." She tried to look back, remember what Nate had said about leaving and why he was going. But she couldn't think straight. All she knew was he wasn't what she thought he was. "How could I know?"

"It's no secret, Shara. My God! Two months ago I had a spread in *Life*. Didn't you see it?"

She took another step away from him. "I don't get *Life*!" After a pregnant pause she asked, "What about the last month? You haven't been away, have you?"

He looked as if he was trying to be patient. "Nothing came up. I don't do this on a schedule. I don't understand why you're so upset."

He actually didn't. He had no idea. Well, she'd have to make it perfectly clear. "I had a father who didn't care I was born, a stepfather who considered everything more important than me, and a husband who thought it was my duty to sit home and wait for him. These past couple of weeks I thought I'd finally met a man who cared about family and a home and a settled life. But you don't. Chasing adventure comes first and always will. And if you think I'm going to expose myself and Danny to that, you've got another thought coming."

She dropped her angry gaze, but her voice was filled with determination. "You'd better take me home."

"I thought we were going to dinner!" He had to keep her with him and talk this through. He couldn't absorb everything she said, but he knew he didn't want her walking out of his life.

"You're acting as if nothing's wrong. *Everything's* wrong. I can't see you anymore. I can't get attached and then you'll be . . . you'll be gone. To California, or Kalamazoo, or Iceland. Don't you understand? I can't do that to me and I can't do that to Danny."

He wouldn't let her cut the thread that tied them together. "I can't believe you're serious. We've found something special. Don't throw it away."

"No," she said emphatically. "Better we end this now before we both get hurt. Please take me home, Nate."

He looked into her eyes, seeing the sorrow and sadness. There was nothing he could say at that moment to change her mind.

Nate drove Shara home in silence. She didn't give him the chance to get out of the van and walk her to the porch. Before he could unbuckle his seat belt she said, "Good-bye, Nate," jumped out of the van, and walked quickly to her door. She went inside without a backward glance.

SIX

Nate hurried through the Harrisburg Airport, his camera equipment slung over one shoulder, his overnight bag cutting into his hand. The job was done. Mason would be happy with what he was getting. Nate's instincts, judgment, and experience put him a notch above other photojournalists. His perception told him when to stay, when to go, when to get out. It had never failed him. But something strange had happened. The assignment in Pittsburgh had lost its gloss when Shara left his van. He'd photographed the destruction of two trains colliding. He'd suited up in the clean-up crew's equipment to move in closer and capture the details. He'd investigated the cause, whether the accident originated in the control room or with the engineer. He'd talked to officials afraid the bromine would seep into the water supply. And through it all, he'd thought about Shara, her dismay and surprise, her reaction. Consequently, the assignment hadn't given him the usual rush. What was wrong with him? Could a woman make this much difference?

Nate wended his way through the lounge area of the airport. He navigated around clots of people, more intent on his thoughts than where he was walking. He and Shara had shared two significant events—the death of her husband and the birth of her son. Did the bond he felt for her and Danny stem from that? Or was it more? Was it Shara herself? He didn't know. But he wanted time to find out. He had to persuade her to give it to him . . . give it to *them*.

Just because he traveled didn't mean he didn't care. Sure, he was afraid of settling down, afraid of losing something that kept him vital, strong, spiritually alive. But that didn't mean he couldn't care about her. That didn't mean they couldn't . . . enjoy each other. If anything, it could add to the anticipation between them, the joy they'd share when they *could* be together.

He had to make her understand that what he did was important to him and to the public. He'd been tempted to call her, but decided she could hang up too easily. He was going to confront her face-to-face, and they were going to talk whether she wanted to or not.

The grocery cart's wheels refused to go in the right direction as Shara pushed it ahead of her through the bakery section of the supermarket. Usually the delicious smells stopped her and she picked up a cheese danish or a few raisin bagels. But the last few days she had lost her appetite. Even the aroma of freshly baked sticky buns didn't tempt her. She picked up a loaf of bread and absently dropped it in her cart.

As she wheeled in front of the delicatessen and took a number, Nate popped into her thoughts as he had all week. She missed him. Oh, how she missed him. But she told herself she had taken the only possible road. She couldn't compete with challenge and adventure. The feelings of loneliness and rejection from her childhood never quite disappeared. When she'd sat by herself waiting for Jim to come home, they'd haunted her. She wouldn't let them surface again. Pursuing a relationship with Nate would be begging for heartache. Too much was at stake, including her son's future.

She gave her order to the clerk at the counter when her number was called. She was putting a container of potato salad and a package of ham into her basket when a voice behind her said, "That's not enough for a picnic."

She could pick that voice out of a crowd of a hundred people. She'd never thought she'd hear it now in the Superfresh grocery store. Nate was at her elbow with an empty cart of his own.

"Since when do you do your shopping in this store?" As much as she wanted to cuddle up in Nate's arms and welcome him home, she had to remain firm.

"Since I've been away and returned safe, sound, and hungry. Since I stopped at your place and found Amber watching Danny so you could shop. By the way, I didn't have to beat the information out of her, she gave it freely."

Shara mumbled something unladylike under her breath and gave Nate a look that could send a lesser man running.

He grinned. "What can I say? She likes me."

Shara pushed her cart briskly toward the produce. Nate kept pace beside her. She tore a plastic bag from the roll above the counter, tested the firmness of the loose peaches, and put four in a bag.

Nate crossed his cart in front of hers to block her path.

"Add some grapes and cantaloupe and we can make a fruit salad to take along tomorrow."

"Tomorrow?"

"I'm going to play hooky and take you and Danny to Caledonia State Park for the day."

He looked smug, self-satisfied, sexy, and appealing all at the same time. "Nate, I told you I can't see you—"

He crossed her lips with his finger. "Didn't Mrs. Pennington teach you never to say 'can't'?"

When Shara merely glared, he ran his finger over her upper lip. Her heart somersaulted and her resistance began to melt. He was so damn sexy, friendly, caring. She didn't know what to do. She didn't want the pain, but she didn't know how to say good-bye, either.

He seemed to sense her confusion. When someone's cart brushed by him, he muttered, "We're blocking traffic. I need food like I need a new camera lens. Shara, we have so much to talk about. Don't run away from me. Hear me out. I'll let you alone now if you promise to go to Caledonia with me tomorrow. I'll pick you up around ten. We can eat a picnic lunch and come home whenever we want."

When Shara had wanted to talk with Jim about their problems, he would brush her off and find something more important to do. Didn't she owe it to Nate to listen? She made a decision. "Okay. We'll go with you tomorrow. But I'm not going to change my mind about how I feel."

"You'll listen with an open mind?"

"It's not my mind I'm worried about. It's my heart." Somehow he'd backed her into a corner and she felt as if she'd have to battle her way out.

His gray eyes were alive with feeling. "I know. I'm asking you to trust me."

All the fight left her. "You realize with Danny along, we'll have to practically take the kitchen sink."

His grin rivaled the Cheshire cat's. "No problem. You gather everything you need, I'll get it there."

Nate pushed his cart into a vacant corner at the end of a shelf stacked with sacks of potatoes. He came back to Shara and tenderly caressed her cheek. "I'll see you tomorrow morning."

Before Shara had a chance to say good-bye, Nate placed a light kiss on her lips and left her in the middle of the produce department.

The heat wave had broken and eighty degrees seemed like a balmy spring day. During the two-hour drive to the state park, Danny was awake, so Shara concentrated her attention on him. She sat in the backseat next to him, playing with his fingers and toes and generally keeping him happy.

In the middle of the week, the parking lot at Caledonia was almost deserted. Shara and Nate found a table along the stream away from the swimming pool and other visitors. The water softly splashed over gray-and-brown rocks, inviting bare feet as Shara sat on the bench holding her son. Beyond the stream lay a field dotted with wild daisies.

Nate made three trips from the van. The last thing he carried to their picnic site looked like a collapsed crib with a lid.

He set it up, watching Shara's expression. "It's a few inches off the ground so no dampness seeps in and the net sides keep out bugs." He put the lid on the top. "Nothing can get in from this way, either."

"Nate, you shouldn't have bought that. You're acting as if . . ."

He waited for her to finish.

"As if you have to take care of us. I can't keep accepting—"

"We'll talk about it along with everything else *after* our walk."

She didn't know why he was postponing the inevitable. "Nate."

He ignored her tone and unfolded what looked like a canvas bag with straps. Hanging it over his head, he held out his hands for Danny. "With this he can be safe, close, and go anywhere we go."

Shara knew the safety of being held against Nate's chest. She had no worries about Danny. Surrendering for the time being, she asked with resignation, "Where do you want to walk?"

He grinned with satisfaction, caught his camera from the bench, and hung it around Shara's neck. She looked down at the expensive piece of photographic equipment. "You trust me with this?"

Nate patted Danny's rump. "You trust me with this?"

She had from the moment Danny was born. "Yes, I do."

Nate caught her hand. "Enough said."

They walked toward the nature trail with easy familiarity, greeting passersby. As soon as they entered the sanctuary of the prepared trail, the smell of sun-baked pine surrounded them. Their steps were silent on the carpet of pine needles and leaves that cushioned their steps. A blue jay warned his relatives of their approach. Sunlight sprinkled through elm leaves making patterns where Shara walked. Nate reached for his camera, and minutes later they entered a clearing. The silence was churchlike. When Nate heard a sound, he lifted his camera. Two chipmunks scurried by and Shara heard the shutter click twice in succession. They soaked in the silence for a few moments, then continued walking.

Laurel banked the trail. Spying a full pink-and-white bloom on a branch, Nate plucked it and put it in Shara's hair. He ran his finger around her ear, down her neck. Shara tried not to react, but goose bumps broke out along her arms. Nate was trying to bind her to him and he was doing a good job.

Danny began to wiggle restlessly so they hurried along to the end of the trail. By the time they returned to the picnic site, he was whimpering. Shara took a bottle out of the cooler and Nate went to warm it under the hot water in the bathroom while Shara changed Danny. After she fed him, she laid him in the port-a-crib.

Nate stood looking down at Danny. Shara watched the warm lights in Nate's eyes as he looked down at her child. They were bonding. She could see it; she could feel it.

When the baby seemed settled, Nate put the lid on the crib. "Do you want to have our lunch on the table or over by the tree?"

"By the tree." Fetching a blanket and the jug of lemonade from the table, she carried them to the picnic area.

When she spread out the blanket, Nate put the cooler on one corner. As he pulled out a bucket of fried chicken, Shara sighed. They were going to eat before they talked.

Nate avoided the subject of his trip to Pittsburgh as they ate. Shara laid out her outline for the articles she was planning for the *Herald*.

Nate sipped the last of his lemonade and put down his cup. Leaning against the tree trunk, he crossed his long legs in front of him. "Do you still want to kick me out of your life?"

Unconsciously, Shara toyed with the flower lodged behind her ear. "I don't know how to make you understand."

"I do understand." When she looked dubious, he sat up straighter, forgetting the relaxed pose. "But I think you're wrong to cut us off before we begin. I can't make any promises. My life is what it is. But what's wrong with living today for today and making the most of it? Aren't two weeks a month better than none? Sometimes I don't travel for a couple of months at a time."

When his stockpile of persuasion didn't seem to work, he aimed straight for the core. "Won't you be sorry if you run away without trying?"

Her breathing quickened. She wasn't a quitter. She never ran away. Did having a baby make her more cautious, afraid to grasp life? To avoid the answers, she asked, "Why do you have to do it? Why can't you be satisfied with the newspaper? What does roaming the world give you?"

"Freedom. Challenge. Excitement."

"Escape," she said bitterly. "If anything gets too heavy or stressful, you take off."

His brows drew together fiercely. "That's not true! I take my responsibilities seriously and I don't shirk them." After a significant pause, he said with slow firmness, "I'm not Jim Nolan."

She backed off. "Okay. So your work makes you feel good."

"And creative, and validated. It's my career." His voice carried a wealth of feeling—resolve, purpose, love for his profession. "Why did you go to Bolivia, Shara?

What made you decide on public health? What makes you work with people instead of sitting in an office pushing papers around?"

"My career's different from yours."

He moved closer to her as if their proximity would help her understand. "I can make a difference. I can do what few men are willing to do. It's a calling, just like yours. It's a talent. I want to use that talent to the best of my ability, Shara, just as you use yours."

She shook her head. "That's not the issue. I don't want to become attached to you, Nate. I don't want Danny to become attached to you. Not when there's a chance you'll take off one day and not come back because you've found someplace or someone more exciting."

He was gruff. "I can't give up who I am. I want to experience life every way I can, to taste adventure when the adventure's worth chasing."

The silence between them was deafening. Water rippling, birds chirping, a faraway voice didn't alleviate it. Nate took her hand and kissed her knuckles. "And as far as finding a woman more exciting, you don't have to worry about that. You're the first woman who's made me think about why I do what I do. My life's my own. I've never defended my comings and goings. I don't want to now, but I want to make you understand."

She looked away from him into the stream. When she faced him again, her emotions were mixed. "I don't understand."

His fingers slipped from her elbow down her arm to her wrist. "Give us a chance. Maybe you'll come to understand."

Tears brimmed in Shara's eyes. He was asking her to

put her dreams of stability aside. They were old dreams she couldn't let go of easily.

He brushed her hair away from her face and laid his hand along her cheek. "Are you willing to try?"

Falling in love with Nate would be a risk, but she already had so many strong feelings for him. She couldn't fathom sending him out of her life. She braced her hand on his chest, longing to touch him more intimately, yet afraid to. "I'm scared."

"I know. I have a few fears myself. But I don't want to stop seeing you."

Her words were low and thready, almost inaudible. "I don't want to stop seeing you, either."

His arms encircled her and his lips came down on hers before she could change her mind.

The desire in Nate's kiss was consuming. His lips demanded she respond. She felt his body tense and harden as he stretched out beside her. His arms were a strong band around her, his lips a scorching source of pleasure, his tongue a cogent instrument of escalating intimacy. She felt his arms loosen and she wanted to protest. But then she realized his hands could be more persuasive. They gently stroked her cheeks and neck while he deepened their kiss.

Desire pulsed through Nate. Desire that didn't want to wait. He had been keeping his feelings in check, but now he let the sexual vibrations course through his body. The kiss grew longer, more intense, explosive, as his hand cupped her breast. The gentle pressure made her breast swell until her blouse pulled taut. His thumb found her nipple and rubbed back and forth. He felt more than heard her moan and he did it again.

His thighs felt as if they encased a bonfire. Even as

a teenager with roiling hormones, he hadn't known this intensity. Sheer longing engulfed him, a longing to create in reality the fantasy he'd had for months. His knee separated her legs and sought to provide friction that would satisfy her.

Hot desire expanded from Shara's breasts to between her thighs. Her fingers climbed up Nate's shoulders but were frustrated by the knit material. She wanted to touch his heat and become a part of him. Her hands danced down his chest, found the hem of his shirt, and burrowed underneath. He was so hard, so masculine, so strong. When her hand passed over his stomach, he shuddered.

She clung to him and arched against his knee. Desire exploded, shooting through her body. Her hands went around his back under his shirt and she pulled him on top of her. He smelled like pine and sun and man. She wanted to rub her nose against his skin, play her fingers in intimate places, enclose him with her body. She wanted him so badly. Like a jungle floor sucking her into quicksand, her passion swamped her and she didn't care.

Her hands slid inside his back waistband, dipped and touched taut, hot skin. It wasn't enough. On a journey of their own, her hands left his back and slipped around to the front. She cupped him and, with his moan of approval, fondled and stroked. Her fingers found the snap on his shorts. But when it popped open, the sound startled her.

What was she doing? Seducing Nate in the state park? Good Lord, she shouldn't be doing this. She shouldn't be doing anything like this. Not until she was sure. Not until she knew whether or not they had a future. Her hands dropped away from him and she froze.

Nate felt her withdrawal immediately. "Shara, what's wrong?"

"We've got to stop this, Nate. Now. I can't do this. We can't do this." She heard the panic in her voice. She'd almost done something foolish, as foolish as the night she and Jim . . .

Nate's ragged breath brought her attention back to him. His body was stiff, demanding, and she knew he was having a tough time maintaining control. God, she was so embarrassed. How could she have gotten them into this?

"Give me a minute to cool down," he said hoarsely.

She lay perfectly still, afraid to move. She could feel her cheeks flaming. Was he going to hate her for this? It seemed like hours until Nate rolled to his side, sat up, and raked his hand through his hair.

His jaw was tense, his features hard. "Is it Jim? Do you feel some kind of loyalty—?"

Her embarrassment forgotten, she sat up quickly and touched his arm. "That's not it, Nate—not at all."

He clenched his fists as if the physical action could stop the emotions he was feeling. "You were married to him, you loved him, you had his baby."

She gripped his arm tighter. "I was divorcing him." When her words had no effect, she squeezed it hard. "Will you listen to me?"

The muscle under his cheekbone twitched. His eyes went to her hand on his arm. "I'm listening."

"There are leftovers from my marriage to Jim." When Nate's mouth tightened into a slash, she said, "But not what you think. We had problems. A lot of problems. I don't know if I caused them or he did or if we were just a match that didn't belong together. We separated because we didn't know what else to do. A lot of feelings were dead by then. They are not the problem now."

Nate's expression changed, became less controlled and

more natural. "Did you stop me because you're not ready?"

She felt a flush creep from her neck to her forehead. "Physically, I'm ready." She paused and then decided to be completely honest. "But I have to be sure Danny and I are important to you. I can't take second place to a career—not again." She looked down at her knees. "Besides, I'm not protected."

He took her chin in his palm. "Okay. Message received. But don't think this relationship can stay platonic much longer."

He was right. She'd have to make a decision. Soon. They were too combustible together.

He studied her flushed face, the sparkle of passion still lingering in her eyes. "Pose for me."

She blinked her eyes at his quick change of subject. "What?"

Nate lifted the hair from her shoulder and let it stream through his fingers. She had so many dimensions, so many colors, qualities that were elusive yet vibrant. He wanted her to light on his hand like a beautiful butterfly. He wanted her to belong to him, to have her touch him with all her beauty.

"I want you to pose for me. Change into your bathing suit. We'll get some sun and take some pictures in the stream along the bank."

"You're serious?" When he nodded, she bargained, "I'll pose if you teach me how to take good pictures. I want to get a camera so I'll have a log of Danny growing up."

"I have some cameras lying around the dark room."

"Nate . . ."

He read her intonation as clearly as bold-faced print and

lifted his hands in surrender. "Okay. You buy your own."
He wiggled his brows teasingly. "But until then, you can
borrow one of mine."

Shara stood and brushed her hands across her seat.
"You're impossible, Nathan McKendrick."

He stood up and gave her a quick, hard kiss. "Not
impossible. Full of possibilities."

"Danny could wake up any time," she warned.

With his customary acceptance of the baby's schedule,
he replied, "If he does, we'll dangle his toes in the
stream. He'll love it."

Shara changed into a one-piece emerald-green suit while
Nate stayed with Danny; then she waited while Nate
changed. When he walked toward her with his clothes
folded over his arm, she felt her blood run hot. He was
so darn sexy in a rugged, self-confident but unpretentious
way. Her eyes skimmed the edges of his sleek black
trunks. He was beautifully made, a study in male land-
scape—mature, powerful muscles, strong tendons, hills
and valleys that were supremely masculine.

Nate dropped his clothes on the bench of the picnic
table and slipped off his moccasins. He picked up his
camera and Shara joined him at the edge of the stream,
her heart almost stopping when she looked into his eyes.

He held his camera almost lovingly with an easy maneu-
vering that proved it had been a best friend over the years.
He snapped picture after picture as Shara stepped over
rocks and stooped to examine pretty pebbles.

Nate made his way over to her. She looked so damn
provocative with her head tilted in the sunlight, her green
eyes sending him mixed messages because of her doubts.
She was so very feminine. He loved watching her with

Danny. He loved watching her, period. When she looked up, he snapped another shot.

All of a sudden she said, "Show me how to take a good picture."

He handed her the camera. "What do you want to take a picture of?"

Her hair blew in the warm breeze. "Besides you?"

"I could blow up a picture of myself in a swimsuit and you can hang it in your bedroom."

She narrowed her eyes and took a prolonged tour of his body as if evaluating it. With a coy smile she asked, "You don't want me to get any sleep, do you?"

"I could make a suggestive comment—"

She playfully punched his shoulder. "You know you look good enough to be a poster idol. Now give me a photography lesson."

He caught her in his arms and held her fast. "Whom would you choose? Me or Patrick Swayze?"

She patted his cheek. "I'll have to think about it."

He sighed dramatically and dropped his arms. "Camera lesson number one. Choose your subject."

She pointed to an area of the stream where the water splashed over a large rock in an opalescent sheen.

Nate knew how to see sharp focus quickly; he didn't have to wait for it. But the skill was difficult to teach. "You want to keep the background simple. You don't want the bank and those branches. When you think you have the subject in view the way you want it, take a step closer." When Shara did, he asked, "Where's the sun?"

It was shining directly in front of her. "Where should it be?"

"To your back or to the side."

She readjusted her position.

Nate fixed the f-stop and gave back the camera. "To hold it steady, take a breath, then squeeze the shutter button."

Shara snapped the picture. "That was easy enough. What should I remember when I take pictures of Danny?"

The sunlight was flirting with Shara's hair, exposing red highlights. He tried to concentrate on her question. "Get in close and catch the action. Give him something to play with and the picture will be more fun."

When she handed back the camera, he said, "I'll put this on the table and we can catch crayfish." He set the camera in the shade and grabbed two styrofoam cups, motioning for Shara to join him as he stooped down over a pool of quieter waters.

She gingerly made her way over the stones, trying not to slip. Nate had overturned a rock and was running the cup along the bottom of the stream as something tan and crawly squirmed for cover. "Is there a purpose behind this?" she asked.

He held up the cup like a trophy. "Pure fun. Look what I caught."

Nate's broad shoulders blocked the sun. She peeked into the cup and screwed up her nose. "Your idea of fun and mine must be different."

He threw her a mischievous glance. "I'm sure we could find mutual grounds for agreement."

She watched the play of his shoulder muscles as he stooped over with the other cup. She wanted to wrap her arms around him, snuggle into his neck, and kiss him. But she couldn't. Not until she decided if he could play a role in her life.

To get her mind off their physical attraction, she cupped

her hands, scooped up water, and splashed it down Nate's neck and back.

The cold water startled him and he lost his balance, landing on his tush, his legs spread in front of him. "Why you little vixen! If you'd rather play in the water instead of catching crayfish, I'll give you a run for your money."

As he started to get to his feet, she backed up slowly. "Now, Nate. Your back looked hot. I was merely trying to cool you off."

"Cool me off? I think you need to be cooled off, too. Your bathing suit's not even wet!"

She backed up farther as he stalked her. "It looks much better dry. Believe me. You wouldn't like it wet."

His hands reached out to grab her waist. "You'll look great dripping. The material clinging . . ." His long arms caught her before she could retreat and he swung her up into his arms. She let out a squeal as he set her down with a splash in the middle of the stream.

"I don't believe you did that!" she sputtered. "I didn't mean to get you all wet. I just wanted—"

"To cool me off. So you said." He sat down beside her in the water and pulled her across his lap. "When I'm with you, it'll take more than cold water."

His touch, his words, his manhood growing beneath her, made her feel desirable, made her irreversibly aware that he was a man and she was a woman. She sighed, "Oh, Nate," and willingly vined her arms around his neck. She didn't have time to breathe before his lips ambushed hers and she gave herself up to the joy of the moment.

SEVEN

Nate slipped into the conference room at the Holiday Inn unnoticed. Shara stood at the podium in front of the room in a bright red linen suit. Her hair was intricately braided and wrapped in a coronet around her head. His body reacted to her loveliness. For a man who knew how to keep his cool in practically any situation, he sure was having serious problems with his reactions whenever he was near her.

Her decision to give this seminar surprised him. She was so wrapped up in Danny, he'd assumed she didn't want to think of work until September. Nate watched as she led the group in a progressive relaxation technique. Her voice was strong and confident. The group responded to her, following her directions, relaxing their bodies to alleviate symptoms of stress. He'd seen her use the same method with his employees and was glad she'd taken this opportunity to stay involved professionally.

Finishing the visualization, she wrapped up the session.

She hadn't seen him and he was glad because he didn't want her to feel self-conscious. The conference attendees stood and he lost sight of her. As he moved forward, he saw she was talking to a good-looking guy who could model for a toothpaste ad. Nate was startled by the tension coiling in his stomach.

He moved closer and heard the man ask, "Do you do private sessions?"

Shara didn't look perturbed or offended. "Not usually. Most of this kind of work can be done in groups."

The man took a step closer to her until his shoulder brushed hers. "But biofeedback has to be learned one-on-one, doesn't it?"

"Yes."

"So will you give me a private appointment?"

Her voice stayed friendly though firm. "Mr. Lascow, I'm taking a temporary leave of absence. I did the seminar today as a favor for a friend."

"And for the money?" he asked in a joking manner.

She smiled. "It doesn't hurt."

"I'd pay you well."

"I'm sure you would, but I don't have time to take on private clients. Many psychologists these days employ biofeedback. I can send you a few names if you'd like. I don't have them with me."

Lascow's charming smile turned Nate's stomach. This joker wasn't interested in biofeedback any more than Danny was. Couldn't Shara see that?

Lascow took a business card from his inside coat pocket and handed it to Shara. "I'd appreciate the information. You're sure you're not interested?"

She nodded. "Positive."

"If I can't hire you to teach me to relax, maybe you

could help it happen by going to dinner with me." His expression was hopeful, his eyes gleaming a message Nate would have liked to knock out of his head.

"Thank you for the invitation, but I'm not dating right now. My son takes up my time and attention."

Nate couldn't believe her composure. He was losing his. Not dating? What were he and Shara doing? Playing brother and sister? His jaw locked.

Lascow was speaking again. "You have my card if you change your mind. Don't hesitate to call."

Shara gave him another nod then picked up her notes on the table. Lascow moved away with a long last look.

Nate touched Shara's arm and she jumped. "Oh, hi! I didn't see you."

"Obviously. You were pretty engrossed." He tried to keep his face emotionless, his voice tempered.

"Excuse me?"

"Lascow. Why didn't you brush him off?"

She stared at Nate curiously. "I did. If you were eavesdropping, you heard."

"I wasn't eavesdropping."

"Um." She packed her papers in her briefcase and clicked it shut. "I know better than to alienate potential clients. Contacts are important."

After a pause Nate asked, "Is Amber baby-sitting?"

"No. I found a teenager who—"

"A teenager? You let a kid stay with Danny?"

Shara looked at Nate as if he was someone she didn't know. "I make the decision concerning who keeps my son. Do you have a problem with that?"

He knew he didn't have rights where she and Danny were concerned. Suddenly he wished he did. What had gotten into him? Uncomfortable with her tone and his reaction, he snapped, "Can you take time for lunch?"

She picked up her briefcase and held it by her side. "Not if you're going to give me the third degree."

"C'mon." Nate took her hand and pulled her with him.

"Nate! Nate, stop it." She cemented her high heels to the floor and wouldn't budge.

He sighed. "Let's get out of this crowd so we can talk. All right?"

He didn't realize he'd been holding his breath until she nodded and he let it out. He led her to the lobby, not sure what he was going to say. They sat on two curved-back chairs facing each other. Shara crossed her legs and stared at him levelly.

He adjusted his tie. "I'm sorry."

Unfortunately she bypassed his apology and honed in on his behavior. "What happened in there?"

He shifted in his seat, pulling his feet in. "I don't like someone hitting on you."

She rolled her eyes. "It goes with the territory."

"It happens often?"

She shrugged. "Once in a while. It's nothing to get in a tizzy about. I don't know why you are."

There was a rough edge to his words. "Think about it." Before she could, he admitted, "I'm jealous. I don't want anyone else looking at you like that." Or if they did, he wanted the man to know Shara was taken. The realization stunned him. He'd never been possessive about a woman before.

He expected Shara to come back with something like, "We have no claims on each other." Instead, she said, "I guess the important fact is, I'm not looking back."

Her soft-as-silk voice made him wonder if he'd heard

correctly or simply what he wanted to hear. "You told him you weren't dating."

"I'm not. To me dating means playing the field. I'm only seeing you."

His heart melted and he leaned forward to take her hand. "You're a special lady and I'm feeling emotions I haven't felt before. Can you be patient with me?"

"If you can be patient with me."

He'd be patient even if he had to take showers cold enough to turn him blue.

After a slow sweet smile that tightened his groin, she asked seriously, "Do you honestly believe I'd leave Danny with anyone who's not capable? I won't take chances with him, Nate. Jenny came highly recommended. She's seventeen and has two younger brothers and a sister she's helped with since they were born."

Nate ran his thumb over the top of her hand. Her skin was soft, smooth, and he fantasized often about touching and kissing her all over. He needed one of those showers now. *Concentrate on the subject at hand.* "Danny's special to me. He pulls my heartstrings the way Brad did when he was a baby. I took responsibility for Brad then, I feel responsible for Danny now. Maybe it's because I saw them both come into the world."

"I appreciate everything you've done for us."

"I don't want appreciation."

"What do you want?"

"You know what I want." When she couldn't seem to find her voice to answer, he said, "But in the meantime, you can do something else for me."

"What?"

"I'm having a gallery opening in Philadelphia next

weekend. Will you go with me and stay overnight? I'll get separate rooms, but I'd like you by my side.''

"I'd love to go. But . . . I guess I could ask Amber to baby-sit.''

He held her gaze and tried to draw out her feelings. "Are you sure you won't mind leaving Danny? We'll only be gone from Saturday afternoon to Sunday afternoon.''

"I know Danny will be fine with Amber. How long have you been planning this? A gallery showing doesn't happen overnight.''

He sighed with relief. She wanted to go. "The owner of the gallery has been after me for the past few years. I kept putting him off.'' Nate followed his gut instincts most of the time. He didn't let anyone push him into anything that went against the grain. "The time seemed right.''

"I haven't seen many of your photographs.''

"You can look through the negatives anytime, but they're not the same as the full-blown prints. I'd like you at the gallery—to see that part of me.''

She seemed pleased he was trying to make her familiar with all aspects of his life. "Are gallery openings highbrow? Do I need a long gown?''

"You're asking me?'' He chuckled. "From the few I've been to, anything goes. But I would like to take you to a posh restaurant afterward.''

Shara looked like a little girl who was just given her favorite chocolate bar. "I haven't bought a new dress in ages. This is going to be fun.''

"You'll look terrific in whatever you wear.'' His voice had gone to low and intimate without his intending it to.

A small silence brimming with sensual vibrations zinged back and forth between them. The slow ache that had begun the first day he met her was swelling and becoming a constant distraction. "Will you join me for lunch if I promise not to get jealous if the waiter flirts with you?"

When she leaned forward, her perfume teased his senses. "Absolutely. Relaxation makes me hungry."

Nate wondered if making love did, too.

True to his word, Nate reserved two separate rooms in a hotel not far from the gallery where his photographs would be displayed. He pointed out the Silven Gallery to Shara on their way to the hotel.

After Nate adjourned to his room to dress for the evening, Shara admired the sumptuousness of her room. It was beautifully equipped in shades of aqua and rose with Louis XIV furnishings, antique satin curtains, and a king-size bed.

She was touching pink lipstick to her lips when there was a rap on her door. She peered out the peephole and saw Nate. She opened the door. He strode in and whistled in appreciation.

His eyes lingered on the narrow straps of the black silk jersey, dawdled on the wide turquoise sash, the wide strip of turquoise surrounding the full hem. His gaze returned to her face and the upswept hair.

His voice was husky. "You are beautiful."

She heated up under his avid approval. Nothing had prepared her for Nate's appearance in a tux. The coat matched the blackness of his hair. The starched white shirt emphasized his bold features and tanned skin. The stripe up the length of his trousers made his legs look endless. He was magnificent. So magnificent she wasn't sure she knew him. Until he walked up to her, took her in his arms and kissed her so hard she thought she'd faint—not from lack of air but from the sheer longing to become a part of him.

Raising his head, he said sheepishly, "I messed up your lipstick."

She smoothed her thumb over his upper lip. "You might have more on than I do." She snatched a tissue from the dresser and handed it to him. "We can both repair the damage." She grinned at him impishly. "Unless you want to do it again."

He looked over at the king-size bed. "If we do it again, we might not get out of here tonight."

Involuntarily, her eyes followed his to the bed. She turned to the mirror above the dresser, but her hand was shaking as she reapplied the lipstick. When she finished, she turned to Nate. He was staring absently out the window, jiggling the loose change in his pocket.

Walking up behind him, she put her hand on his shoulder. "Nate? You're not nervous, are you?"

"Who, me?"

His vulnerability touched her. He was usually so self-assured, so in charge. "You have nothing to worry about, you know. Your work's exceptional."

His glance was skeptical. "You haven't seen much of it."

"I've seen enough to know your photography is art," she calmly assured him removing her hand from the tux. "Why else would a gallery want to show your work?"

He twitched his already perfectly knotted tie into a better position. "I don't know what the reviewer will say. I feel the pictures I take show truth and beauty. If he doesn't like my truth . . ."

She brushed his hand away from his tie and straightened it. "Are you proud of your work?"

He stood stock-still. "Of course I am."

"That's all that matters."

His gray eyes combed hers as if they were searching for something. "You're good for me."

There was an energy about Nate, a sense of purpose yet a sense of fun. He had lived life hard and knew how to appreciate it. She needed that. "As good as you are for me." She brushed her fingers over his lapel. "I hope Danny's all right with Amber."

"She takes good care of him."

Nate never told her to stop worrying. He just reassured her, so the worry evaporated naturally. Shara gave him a hug. "Let's go make that reviewer write the best review of his life."

The owner of the gallery had engaged a limousine for Nate so he didn't have to battle traffic. When they arrived at the gallery and stepped over the threshold, Warren Silven, a short, wiry man with an abundance of energy, welcomed Nate and suggested he circulate. Shara and Nate became separated so she moved about on her own, eager to view Nate's work.

Each picture was different, a masterpiece of its own. Shara examined a photo that was shot into the sun. The sparkle of water and light glanced off the backs of dolphins poised in midair. There was a series of night pictures—streetlights flaring into bright stars, designs of light and dark against buildings, shadows and silhouettes coming to life with eerie images. One photo caught expressions of intense feeling on a group of student demonstrators. Another series captured the predicament of a child attempting to master the art of eating spaghetti. Shara had to laugh.

There was a picture of a hot dog vendor forking sauerkraut onto a frank. He looked so real, he could have been standing in front of Shara and she'd notice no more detail.

Suddenly she felt an arm around her shoulders and Nate was beside her asking, "What do you think?"

"I think there's more life in your photographs than most people see on the street. How do you do it? Look at this man. I can reach out and touch the lines on his face!"

"I talk to everyone I photograph. If they're involved in conversation, they don't freeze. A good photograph tells how the subject feels or how the photographer feels about the subject. This man loves life. He loves standing on a corner in New York City selling hot dogs and meeting more people in a day than some folks meet in a lifetime."

One element Shara noted in all Nate's pictures. There were contrasts—light and dark, old and young, beautiful and stark. One emphasized the other and made none of the pictures mundane.

She pointed to a sequence of lightning striking through a black sky. "How did you do that?"

He shifted his gaze from her to the photographs. "That was taken from my terrace. I set the camera on time exposure on a tripod during a storm. I left the shutter open for about twenty minutes. That's what I got."

As Shara walked along the aisle and studied the series on the children of Ethiopia, they grabbed her heart. A picture of homeless men on a street corner in the dead of winter did the same. Besides artistic talent, there was deep emotion in the pictures.

She stopped and asked, "Your camera is your eye, isn't it?"

"It's better. It remembers the image and gives it back." His arm gestured to the photographs along with the people in the room who were laughing, talking, and looking. "It can take from confusion what is exciting and beautiful. Life is a design. With a camera, I can freeze the design and remember it later. Come over here. There's a special photograph I want you to see.''

In a corner of the gallery, mounted by itself, was a photograph of Shara and Danny. It had been taken at Caledonia. Late-afternoon light brought out the glow on Shara's face as she looked down at her son. Her hair was a glossy backdrop and contrast to the pink baby face and his tiny hand reaching for her cheek. The light behind her head created a strong outline.

Tears sprang to her eyes. Nate had said his pictures told truth. This picture portrayed the love between Shara and her child, but also the feeling Nate held for both of them. Why was she resisting making love with him? His assignments seemed to be a remote issue, light years away.

Nate caught the tear that escaped and trickled down her cheek. ''What's wrong?''

''It's so beautiful, Nate. It makes me realize how you see me and Danny. I feel . . . honored.''

His stance relaxed perceptibly. ''I was afraid you might not want it on display. But it was so special, I sent it to Silven before I thought about it. Of course, it won't be sold. That's mine to keep.''

Their eyes were communicating secret messages when a burly elderly man with a cigar in his mouth clapped Nate on the shoulder. ''Congratulations, McKendrick. Quite a showing you've got here.''

Nate looked surprised. ''Halstein. What are you doing in Philadelphia?''

The glass of champagne in the older man's hand almost spilled when he raised his glass. ''I had some business here and decided I'd stop in.''

Nate introduced Shara. "Guy Halstein, meet Shara Nolan." He explained to Shara, "I do some work for Guy now and then."

A cold shiver prickled between Shara's shoulder blades, but she extended her hand. "It's nice to meet you."

"You too, Ms. Nolan. I see you're the inspiration behind one of McKendrick's works." Halstein took a puff from his cigar and blew the smoke above his head. "I won't interrupt your evening. But could you meet me tomorrow for an hour or so?"

Nate's eyes caught Shara's. "I'm afraid I can't. Our schedule is full. But I'll be glad to drive down to Baltimore and see you next week. I'll call your secretary Monday and she can set something up that's convenient for both of us."

Halstein didn't seem offended. "Fine by me, but the sooner the better." He pointed to a gentleman with a notebook and pen at the other side of the gallery. "Don't worry what he says about the photographs. We both know what your skill is worth." He winked. "It might even be worth more than you imagine."

After Halstein crossed to a group of people he apparently knew, Shara asked, "What's this full schedule we have tomorrow? Don't you think you should have met with him?"

Nate reached into his inside pocket for an imaginary list. He pretended to check it carefully. "Let's see. First item on the agenda is taking you to breakfast. Second, the Liberty Bell and Independence Hall. Then I'm taking you home to your son." He looked up. "Business doesn't fit in. I can see Guy next week."

Shara felt a warm glow around her heart. Nate was

putting her before business. It was a wonderful feeling. She wanted to put her arms around him and hug him close.

Instead she said, "Thank you."

His eyebrows lifted. "For what?"

"For making me feel important to you."

"You *are* important to me, Shara. Very important."

His words sent a trembling need racing through her. The need to lie naked with him, to satisfy the intense yearning she'd never known before.

She stood next to Nate for the remainder of the evening, giving him moral support, waiting for an official verdict. When almost all the patrons had dispersed, the man with the notebook came over to Nate.

"I'm Trent Conrad from the *Philadelphia Inquirer* and I merely want to say, well done, Mr. McKendrick. I've seen your spreads and I was curious to see if you had art in you along with mechanical skill. There's no need for you to wait until tomorrow's *Inquirer* hits the stands. You've got both. I predict the people who bought your photos tonight made a good investment."

The reviewer didn't waste time in idle chitchat. Shaking Nate's hand, he left the gallery. Nate and Shara looked at each other and laughed.

The anticipation, the excitement for Nate, the good review made her feel supercharged. "I told you you had no reason to worry."

"I wasn't worried."

When Shara threw him a glower, he grinned and shrugged. "I have to speak to Silven, then we're getting out of here. I made reservations at Rudolpho's."

Shara felt as if she were moving in a dream. They had use of the limousine for the night. She felt like royalty being chauffeured around the city. But more important, she felt belonging as Nate's arm rested naturally around her shoulders. On the way to the restaurant she realized Nate could be living a life far removed from York, Pennsylvania. As they walked into the four-star restaurant, she wondered how often he had been there before. The maître d' knew him.

After they were seated at a table for two in a secluded corner, she asked, "Why did you decide to have your showing in Philly?"

Nate seemed distracted by her bare shoulders. His eyes moved across them. "This used to be a base. I had an apartment here and called it home between assignments. How do you like the restaurant?"

She looked around at the mirrors, live greenery, and distinctive crystal chandeliers. "I like it very much. We don't have anything like it in York. Don't you miss this type of place?"

"No, I don't." He reached across the table and covered her hand with his. "Eating out is only fun when you have someone to eat with."

Her lips twitched at the corners. "You never had anybody to eat with? I can imagine glamorous women on your arm—"

"Not anybody like you." He squeezed her fingers. "You make the difference."

The current between them when they touched always shocked Shara. She was connected to Nate more powerfully than she had ever been connected to anyone. What would happen if they let the electricity flow?

Checking with Shara, Nate ordered chateaubriand for two. When the waitress left their table, he asked if she would like to dance.

She nodded.

Nate rose and held out his hand. She took it and her pulse quickened.

After they reached the wooden dance floor, his arm slid around her waist, his other hand holding hers flat against the hardness of his chest. Shara gazed up at him. Nate's eyes caressed her until she trembled and laid her head on his shoulder, breathing the musky fragrance of his cologne and rubbing her cheek against the rough fabric of his tuxedo.

Nate's hand played up and down her back sending a rippling sensation percolating through her body, and she found herself matching his motion by gently stroking his neck. She leaned into his arms, felt the muscular pressure of his thighs against hers, the warmth of his breath on her neck, and the staunch firmness of his lean male body against her soft curves. His body responded to her closeness and she felt his arousal. He didn't pull back, but let her know exactly what she did to him. His tongue whispered along the shell of her ear, making her tremble. When it dipped inside, she held on to Nate tightly so she wouldn't lose all sense of reality. She wanted this man. She wanted to make love to him; she needed him to make love to her. Tonight.

They danced until Nate realized the music had stopped. He whispered in Shara's ear, "We're the only ones on the dance floor."

She looked around and when her eyes fell on the saxophone player, the musician winked. A giggle rose to her throat. She stifled it and said, "I think we'd better eat."

At their table, Nate poured the wine and raised his glass in a toast. When she raised hers, he clinked their glasses. "To the present."

"To the present."

They ate slowly, not only appreciating the quality of the food, but the time they were spending together. They didn't make conversation but drank in each other's presence. Nate fed her a bite of meat. Shara offered him a forkful of whipped potatoes. When his lips came around the fork, he held it between his teeth longer than necessary. He released it and licked his lips. His eyes said he desired more than food. Prolonging the meal, they ordered a delicate lemon sorbet for dessert.

Nate finished the last spoonful. "Would you like to dance again?" Holding her in the middle of the dance floor was safe. He couldn't go beyond the limits of propriety.

"I'd rather go back to the hotel," she said quietly.

He was surprised. Maybe she was tired. They had had a full day. Maybe she wanted to call Amber and check on Danny. "Okay."

Nate was puzzled as they rode back to the hotel. Shara was silent, but she wasn't withdrawn. When he hung his arm around her shoulders, she nestled against him as if she belonged. It was just as well if she was tired. She probably wouldn't ask him in. That would prevent the mighty temptation of letting kisses go too far.

They admired the deeply piled mauve carpeting and formal white-and-gold decor of the lobby as they waited for the elevator. The doors slid open and they stepped inside. The doors swooshed shut and they were alone. Nate couldn't prevent his arms from gathering Shara close. His lips coaxed, beguiled, softly roamed from her lips to her cheek to her throat and back up to the highly sensitized hollow of her ear. His tongue teased and tormented. Shara murmured his name and clung to his shoulders.

When the door dinged open, they separated unwillingly. Nate held Shara close as he walked her to her room, not wanting to let her go or say good night but knowing he had to.

They stopped at her door. Shara's smile was shy. "I had a lovely time."

Telling himself again Shara's room was off limits if he wanted to be an honorable man, he said, "We'll have to do this more often."

"It wasn't the limousine, or the restaurant, or the band. It was being with you."

His need for her transcended physical desire. "You know I feel the same way."

"I feel like Cinderella," she confessed. "I don't want the night to end."

He'd better leave fast, before he swept her into his arms and kissed her senseless. "We'll have other nights."

"There's no reason we can't take advantage of this one, is there?"

Her upturned face and the sparkle in her eyes were so damn tempting. "I don't think I should come in. As much as I want to, it could lead to—"

"I want you to come in." She could see he didn't understand and she'd have to say it straight out. "I don't want you to sleep in your room tonight. I want you to sleep in mine."

EIGHT

His astonished expression made her smile. "Does that come as a shock?"

His eyes were smoky gray. "What changed your mind?"

She didn't believe she was doing this, being forward enough to ask a man to sleep with her. But this wasn't just any man. "It's not a matter of changing my mind. That photograph of me and Danny . . . it showed how much you care about us both. It's not fair that you do all the giving."

His voice was rough. "I don't want to be paid back, Shara. I don't see making love that way. If that's your only reason . . ."

His remark surprised and angered her. This wasn't the way this was supposed to turn out. It was difficult enough for her to make the first move. He was acting as if she wanted to trade something, as if he could care less.

She backed off and her tone was chilly. "Forget the whole thing. You go to your room, I'll go to mine."

"If that's what you want." His look was guarded.

She rummaged in her purse for her key and unlocked the door. "I just told you what I wanted and you decided to analyze it to death." She opened her door and stepped inside. "I'll see you in the morning."

"Right. In the morning." He walked away from the door before she closed it. She leaned against it and felt a sob rise to her throat. What had happened? What went wrong? They both wanted to . . .

The rap on the door was so hard she felt it all the way up her spine. When she looked through the peephole and saw Nate, her heart hammered. She opened the door wide.

Nate drew her into his arms and murmured into her hair, "I'm sorry."

Against his shoulder she said, "I don't know what happened."

He let out a long breath. "I've wanted you for so long, I guess I was in shock. I was afraid you thought you owed me something and I don't want that to be the reason . . ."

She pulled back in his arms and took his face between her hands. "I want you, Nate. I want you to make love to me."

He took her hand and led her inside.

Nate's hand was shaking as it went to his tie. He had dreamed of this night for months, and he couldn't believe it was happening. He shucked his jacket and threw it over the chair. Shara was standing at the foot of the bed watching him.

He crooked his finger at her. "Come here." She walked into the circle of his arms. When his lips captured hers, she gave as much as he wanted and more.

Nate's fingers fumbled with the pins holding her hair in place. He took them out one by one, letting them fall to the floor. He ran his fingers through her long hair and tilted her head so his lips had better access.

He broke off the kiss and his voice was strained when he spoke. "If you have any doubts, we can stop right now."

"Oh, I still have doubts. But I won't have any regrets. I want you to make love to me, Nate."

Her words broke his dam of self-restraint. He willed his insides to settle down, not wanting to rush. His knees felt weak with desire and he wondered how he could hold on to his control long enough to make this good for her—so good her doubts would disappear.

Suddenly he remembered something that might postpone their union. "Shara, are you protected? I didn't know we were going to—"

Still sheltered in his arms, she lifted one arm and brushed the back of her hand against his high cheekbone. "It's okay. I saw the doctor last week and I have a diaphragm. There's nothing to worry about."

"Last week, huh?" He grinned.

She blushed but didn't drop her eyes. "Last week."

He slipped his thumbs under the dress straps and pushed them off her shoulders. His lips kissed where the straps had been.

"The zipper," she whispered. "Nate, you have to unhook the zipper."

He released her so she could turn around. While she untied the sash, he pushed her hair aside and kissed her neck with soft, moist kisses. Running the zipper down its track, he followed it with his lips. The dress puddled around her ankles.

Nate unfastened his cummerbund, quickly unbuttoned his shirt, and slipped it off. He unbuttoned his trousers, stripped off his shoes and socks, and stepped out of the briefs and pants. When he stood in front of Shara, his eyes feasted on her shoulders, the lacy cups of her bra, her bare midriff. His body sprang to life.

Shara was staring, without shyness, with appreciation. "Nate, do you *know* what kind of body you have?"

His tone was self-deprecating. "I know that my body's overruling my mind. I know that I've wanted to make love to you since the moment I met you. And I know what's going to happen to my body when you touch me."

"I want to touch you." She reached out and slowly dragged her hand from his collarbone to the edge of his shoulder. "I hope something happens when I do because then I'll know you feel as strongly as I do."

The sexual tension between them was palpable. But there was more, too. So much more. Making love to Shara was going to complicate their relationship. Was he ready? Did this mean some kind of commitment? Tomorrow. He'd think about it tomorrow.

He took her hand, kissed her palm, and led her to the bed. Stretching out on his side, he held his hand out to Shara. "Join me?"

She smiled. "In a minute." She slowly slid the clasp on her strapless bra around to the front. Unhurriedly, she unhooked the catch and let the bra drop. She watched the expression on Nate's face and her smile grew when she saw she was achieving the desired effect. He was immobilized, his body strung with tension.

Sliding her hands into the waist of her black chemise, she wriggled out of it, accentuating the sway of her hips. Only her black translucent panties were left.

As she pulled them down her long legs, Nate's body began to throb and he could feel his cheeks flush. Lord, she made him hot. Hot to his core. How was he going to be able to love her slowly, the way she deserved?

Shara lay down beside Nate, naked and smiling. When he didn't move or react, she brushed her hand up his arm and kissed his shoulder. The tendons along his throat strained as her fingers strolled down his chest. His stomach muscles tightened when she intimately touched his navel and he gasped. She looked up and he gave her a shaky smile. "See what you do to me?"

Her hand trailed down to his thigh and moved closer to his sensitive member.

He groaned. "Shara, if you don't want an explosion—"

"I want an explosion."

"Not before I can give you pleasure."

Her voice was a whisper. "We have all night."

Nate reached for Shara and pulled her tight against him. He kissed her until they were both shaking. He tore away, kissed the tip of her chin, the hollow at her throat. When his breath teased her nipple, it reacted immediately. He rolled it between his lips and flicked it with his tongue. Shara moaned and undulated sensually beside him until he rasped, "Sweetheart, it's going to happen and I can't stop it."

"Don't try," she breathed. She threw her leg across his thighs.

Nate slid her on top of him and guided her hips until he pushed into her warmth. His temperature felt as if it elevated at least ten degrees; his heart accelerated until he lost track of the beats. Searing heat ran through his thighs and he exploded, shuddering with a groan of release, then shuddering again and again.

When he could breathe less erratically, he realized his

eyes were closed. He opened them. "Shara, I didn't want it to happen like that. You didn't—"

She placed her fingers over his mouth, then replaced them with her lips and gave him a long, passionate kiss. His body quivered. Pushing herself up, she moved seductively, ran her hands tauntingly over his chest, and flicked his nipples.

Nate responded to the stimulation. He smiled and said, "Woman, you know me better than I know myself."

Her green eyes locked to his gray ones. "No, not yet I don't. But I will."

"There are going to be more nights like this?" A teasing smile broke across his lips.

With him inside her, with their bodies joined so intimately, she had no choice but to say, "I hope many of them." Her words had the same power as her hands and she smiled at his body's acknowledgment.

Nate pulled Shara down until she braced herself on her elbows. His mouth found her breasts and he suckled, sending waves of pleasure brewing from her nipples to her womb. Her love muscles tightened and released, tightened again to hold him securely. When Nate's hands caressed her spine, she sighed with pure pleasure.

He began thrusting slowly while his tongue laved her breast. The conflagration in Shara began to build. It began as light and airy as a teasing thrill. The sensations began to increase and she slid slightly upward until the friction was exactly where she needed it.

Nate's skin began to shimmer. She was gripping him tightly. Her body became taut, her breathing became a pant. Releasing her breast, he smiled at her pleasure and said, "Let go, sweetheart. Let yourself go."

"You, too. Come with me. I want you with me."

"We're going to fly together." His back arched and he thrust deeper, deeper, until they were no longer two, but one.

When she cried out, he asked anxiously, "Shara?"

"It's wonderful, Nate. Wonderful!"

Her uninhibited tribute pushed him to the edge again. Each thrust propelled him closer to Shara, closer to the peak of perfection. When the final wave hit, he tightened his arms around her as if he'd never let her go.

His moan of utter fulfillment sent Shara rocketing toward the stars where they burst, showering light and heat prickling through every nerve. With Nate's arms a tight band around her, she knew she had found heaven— a heaven made only for the two of them.

Shara's breath was warm against Nate's ear. He opened his eyes, stroked her hair from her cheek, and was amazed by the peace he was experiencing. He had never felt like this before. Never. Once again he heard the bars of a cage rattling. He ignored the sound.

Nate awoke the next morning, finding himself curved into Shara's back, his knees cupped under hers. He couldn't help smiling. They had shared something special. The first time could never be repeated and could never be forgotten. She was such a giving lover. She had given much more than he had, and he wanted to give more. How would she react if . . .

Her bottom was soft against him. So soft he became aroused. It sure didn't take much with her. She must have noticed him in her sleep because she rubbed against him. Nate hardened. Slipping his hand around her, he gently laid his palm against her breast. Her skin was like velvet. He stroked the underside and her nipple puckered. Teasing around the bud but not touching it, he felt the rhythm of her breathing change and he wondered if she was awake. When his fingers finally played with her nipple, she squirmed against him, pressing into him, creating more friction.

Did she ache for him as much as he ached for her? His hand left her breast and while he kissed the nape of her neck, he lingered on the silky brown hair between her thighs. She shifted up toward his hand as if she wanted more. This was a game now, even if she was awake. He wanted to make her hungry for him. He wanted to give her the same pleasure she had given him.

Shara didn't know when she woke up. In her dream, Nate was kissing her, loving her. She was running her hands over his muscles, swirling through his black mat of chest hair. She could feel his touch on her breast, a touch that was creating heat in her most secret places. She could feel his male reaction to her nearness and she wanted to feel more.

His fingers teased her nipple. She tried to keep still but couldn't. She swallowed a moan when his fingers moved lower. They teased at her feminine folds until she thought she'd scream in frustration. Finally, they slid inside, assuaging some of the hunger. She moved against the pressure feverishly seeking a release. Nate teased, loved, praised with his fingers until Shara gave a small cry and fitted herself back against him.

He waited until her breathing was deeper and slower, then kissed her ear, her cheekbone, her eyelid. "Are you awake?"

Shara shifted onto her back. "Nate McKendrick, you know how to wake a woman up." She wrapped an arm around him and snuggled into his shoulder.

"Did you enjoy it?"

She saw the concern in his eyes. "It was a gift. A gift no one has given me before. Thank you." Nate made loving more than physical. They fused spiritually. Even this morning, he had given her a present he couldn't give any other way.

She drew a geometric design on his arm with her finger. "You said you wanted to go sightseeing this morning. Where do you want to go?"

His grin was a flash of pure enjoyment. "Actually, that was before I knew I was going to see much more interesting sights in here."

"You mean I'm in the same category as Independence Hall?" she asked with mock dismay.

He ran his hand down the middle of her back and cupped her buttocks. "Sweetheart, you are in an unmatchable category."

She wiggled suggestively against him. "So you won't be upset if we don't see the Liberty Bell?"

"I'd rather you ring my bell," he teased.

She gently took his manhood in her hand, stroking and fondling until he said raggedly, "Do you know what you're doing?"

"Isn't it the right bell?"

With a growl he caught her close and nibbled on her shoulder. "Let's see how loud we can make it ring."

In the middle of the following week, Nate entered the hospital, hurried through the lobby, and waited for the elevator. The weekend had been more successful than he ever imagined it could be. He felt close to Shara. So close it made him . . . nervous? It was a vague uneasiness—a discrepancy between what he was feeling and how his mind was reacting to being . . . boxed in. Shara wasn't putting any pressure on him, but he felt it was there. Yet he couldn't stay away from her. Like now. Seeing her, being with her even for a short break from work, was almost a compulsion.

He wondered how her morning had gone. She'd come in to investigate what had piled up on her desk, to see if her assistant was having problems coping with the double workload. He knew she didn't want to go back to work yet. She loved taking care of Danny too much. But she was so damn independent. Stubborn was a better word. If she'd just accept some monetary help . . .

Nate exited the elevator and went to Shara's office. Her assistant told him Shara was at the hospital's day-care center. It was a shame they didn't take children under three. She'd love being able to visit Danny a couple of times a day. Hoping the Chinese food he'd brought was piping hot, he searched her out.

As he entered the center, he found her with one glance. She was sitting in a rocker, holding Danny, with four children gathered around her. They looked to be about four to seven years old. As he stepped closer, he realized she was telling them a story.

He listened as she wove the tale about a little girl who traveled to a mysterious land where flowers danced and animals talked. When Shara finished the adventure, one of the girls flung her arms around Shara's neck, giving her a tight hug.

Nate's heart contracted. Did Shara want more children? And if their futures were tied together, what did that mean for him? The idea of having a child with her was inviting. But another child would tie him down more. The more involved he became in Shara's life, the more he felt his freedom slipping away. She had this idea of a family, with the man having a safe nine-to-five job, the woman being able to count on him to be beside her no matter what. Was he capable of giving her that dream? Did he want to try?

Was his desire for a flexible life selfish? For as long as he could remember, he'd resisted putting himself in a situation that closed off his options. They had to be open. Why? Seeing Shara surrounded by children finally told him. He was scared. The same kind of scared as when his father deserted his family. Nate had felt trapped. He'd had no choice but to accept responsibility thrust upon him. Now, it was his choice to accept it or refuse it.

Shara spotted Nate and waved. After she patted a little boy on the head and the kids dispersed, she stood and came toward him. "Maybe I should open a day-care center. Then I could keep Danny at home."

"Your place isn't big enough."

She sighed. "You're right. And I wouldn't make as much as I do here."

Still trying to shove away his serious thoughts, he asked, "How did it go this morning?"

She looked sheepish. "The truth? It felt good to be back. How can I want to do two things at once? Stay home and work?"

He could identify. How could he want a life with Shara and freedom at the same time? "Why don't we go to your office and talk about it? I brought Chinese for lunch. It should still be warm."

She peered down at Danny. "I'll leave him here. The staff wishes they could break the rules and take care of him when I come back."

Nate would prefer stealing Shara away to a nearby motel

and make love all afternoon, but he'd have to wait until tonight. In Shara's office he sat across from her, trying to ignore the floral scent of her perfume, the curve of her lips, and rise and fall of her breasts under her yellow silky blouse.

He spooned sweet-and-sour chicken on top of the mound of rice. "You tell interesting stories."

She glanced at him cautiously, as if she was going to reveal a secret. "When I was a kid, I used to make up fairytales. If I was bored . . . or lonely . . . I'd go to them, live them, be someplace where I felt safe."

Stability and security were so important to her. "Those kids must have identified; they were with you the whole way."

Shara lifted a forkful of rice to her mouth, losing some of it on the way. "They're so adorable. I'd love to have a brood."

His eyes met hers, and for a moment the tension was palpable. "That would be hard to do if you want a career."

She broke their gaze, popped the bite into her mouth and waved the fork dismissively. "I know. But I can dream."

"One of those fairytales?"

"Maybe."

Nate pushed a bite of chicken back and forth on his plate, wondering the best way to broach an issue that had been bothering him for months. "I want to ask you something."

"Go ahead."

He pushed his plate away, his hunger gone. "You might consider it . . . prying, none of my business."

She put her fork down and gave him her full attention. "You can ask."

"You and Jim were going to get a divorce."

"Yes." Her eyes asked where he was going.

Nate restlessly moved back in his seat. "You'd made that decision about three months before Jim died."

"You already know that's true."

He felt vulnerable, like all his defenses were on the line. "Then how was Danny conceived? Why?"

The silence was full, hot, suffocating.

"You're right. It's none of your business."

He gripped the chair's arm. "I want to know anyway."

"Why? What does it matter?" She appeared on guard, wary.

"Because if you still cared about him, if you still had feelings, you might now. I don't want the past affecting the present."

"The past always affects the present. We can't escape it," she said with cool objectivity that removed emotions from the discussion.

"We can make the conscious decision to put it aside and go on. If you can put your marriage with Jim in the past, maybe you could accept my . . . career."

She remained silent.

"*Were* you and Jim thinking about reconciling?"

She pushed her chair away from the desk. "Okay. You want to know what happened. Jim and I always had great sex. One night we got carried away. Period."

"You're lying." As sure as he knew his own name, he knew he was right.

She looked as if he'd slapped her. Nate rose, walked around the desk, and turned her swivel chair to face him. "Tell me what happened."

She tried to turn away, but he pulled her up. She wouldn't look at him, but stared over his shoulder. Her face mirrored such sadness, he wanted to hold her and rock her like she did Danny.

She must have sensed his determination because she began speaking. Her voice took on a faraway quality. "Jim didn't want the divorce. We argued about it until he finally moved out. It wasn't much different with him gone than with him there. He was never around."

Nate wanted to make this simple and quick for his sake as well as hers. "He came home to talk to you? To argue?"

Her laugh was humorless. "No arguing this time. He was conciliatory and charming. He brought roses and wine."

"And how did you feel?"

"Nervous. Determined not to let him change my mind."

"Did you fight?"

"Not exactly."

"Shara—"

"All right!" Her body stiffened and she gave him a look that said she hated telling him this. "I drank wine with him while I listened to his arguments. He kept filling my glass. I was nervous. I just wanted him to leave, so I kept drinking."

"You didn't know what you were doing?"

She didn't seem to hear him. "Jim became . . . amorous. He—"

Outrage exploded inside Nate. "The bastard raped you?"

"No, Nate. He . . . I . . . I said no, but he pleaded with me. He was so upset. He didn't want the divorce; I did. I felt so responsible for the breakup. And we were still married. I should have said no again . . ." A tear rolled down her cheek.

Nate could hate Jim Nolan, curse him for the ways he'd hurt Shara, but that wouldn't help her. He held her tight as she laid her head on his shoulder. "From everything you've told me, you weren't responsible for the marriage not working. You have nothing to feel guilty about, nothing to feel sorry for. You know that, don't you?"

She raised her head and brushed her hair away from her forehead impatiently. "My mind does. But my heart still wonders. That night shouldn't have happened."

"You wouldn't have Danny if it hadn't."

"I know."

He gently pulled her closer. When his lips came down on hers, he wanted to encompass her, protect her, always keep her safe. He coaxed her lips apart and invaded with tender strength. As Shara's hands caressed his neck, he fitted her to his body. Her moan filled his mouth while he rubbed against her.

When he tore his lips from hers, he murmured, "I need you, Shara."

She buried her nose in his shoulder. "I could quit for now and come back tomorrow."

He stroked her hair. "That's a superior idea."

Three days later, Nate sat across from Guy Halstein. "What did you want to talk to me about?"

Guy puffed on the ever-present cigar. "I'm reorganizing *World News Monthly*."

"It's a good magazine." Nate cocked his head and asked with curiosity, "Why change it?"

Guy set his cigar in the ceramic ashtray on his desk.

"Internal problems. Bickering. Back stabbing. Goings on that can ruin an editorial staff. I had to fire Ben Davis."

Nate's brows rose. "He's been with you for years."

"I know and I feel bad about it, but he's been shirking his responsibility. Some kind of midlife crisis. He's running around with a twenty-year-old blonde with bazookas out to here." Halstein indicated a two-foot space in front of him and shook his head as if he couldn't believe the man's foolishness and growing ineptitude. "He's been going through a nasty divorce this past year and I think he's gone off the deep end."

"You couldn't help?"

Halstein scoffed. "I own a magazine. I'm not a social worker."

Nate had known Guy for years. He certainly wasn't socially conscious. He was a self-made shrewd businessman. "So who are you replacing him with?"

"That's just it." Halstein squinted at Nate as he rocked back and forth in his chair. "I can't find what I want. It's a pain in the butt. I put Johnson in Davis's place."

"But Johnson was in charge of the photo department."

"He wants to broaden his horizons. At least that's what he says. I think he's fed up riding herd over Clara. They never got along. Anyway, that's why I wanted to see you. I want you in Johnson's spot. I want you in charge of the photo department. As a bonus, I'll give Clara a raise, give her more responsibility and you can take any meaty assignment you want, anywhere in the world. It's an offer you can't refuse."

Nate sat up straight in his chair. "Now wait a minute. Why would I want to work for you when I own a newspaper?"

"Because you miss the wilder life," Halstein stated

bluntly. "You can't tell me you're happy in York. It's too small to give you—"

Nate jumped in. "It's got forty-five thousand people. It's not a village."

Halstein picked up his cigar and poked it at Nate. "Maybe so. But I think you're sitting in an office more than you want to."

Nate frowned. "I'm gone off and on. Enough so I don't get bored." Though he had to admit being with Shara was as much fun as being in the field.

"Don't you want to be there more? Whenever you'd like? Without waiting for a phone call? You could call the shots and have your pick of the best stories." When Nate didn't answer immediately, Halstein continued, "Men like you don't settle down. Even with a pretty lady. You can't take the chili powder out of chili, you can't take the peanuts out of peanut butter, you can't take the hunger for adventure out of a pro like you."

Nate had to ask himself if Halstein was right. Had he been considering settling down? Staying in one place? Not consciously. But maybe this new intimacy with Shara was working on him in ways he didn't know. That was a terrifying thought.

The man sitting across the desk must have sensed Nate's doubts because he said, "You don't have to give me an answer now. Let it sit. I'm not in any hurry to take somebody new on board. Clara's capable of handling the department for a month at least."

Nate wondered what it would be like to run the department, to fly off to . . . Hell! What would Shara say? Was this going to send her running again?

"This decision could change your future." Halstein directed gruffly, "Give it the month."

NINE

"You'll be flying in, not this weekend, but next weekend." Shara verified her mother's plans, trying to keep her emotions removed.

"That's right. We'll stay in York Saturday and Sunday and leave Monday. Chet wants to drive to his brother's after we see you."

Shara supposed she should be grateful her stepfather was giving her the opportunity to see them at all. "Would you like me to pick you up at the airport?"

"No. We'll rent a car. You know Chet doesn't like to depend on anyone for transportation. If he could fly the plane himself, he would."

She was sure he would. Chet had to be in control of everything, all the time. Especially his wife. "Do you want me to make motel reservations?"

"They're already made."

What if this hadn't been convenient for her? It was simple. She wouldn't see her mother until they visited the United States next year.

Her mother's voice became husky as she said, "Shara, I'm really looking forward to seeing Danny. You know if I could have, I would have been there when he was born. And I'd like to stay longer . . ."

"But what Chet wants, he gets." Damn! She usually tried hard not to let the bitterness seep through.

Her mother didn't argue. "I suppose so. That's the way it's always been, I guess I can't change it now."

That was the first Shara had ever heard her mother admit the marriage wasn't always the way she wanted it. Shara's tone softened. "You can spend as much time as you want with Danny. I'll make sure we're free all weekend."

"Thank you, honey. I have to run now. You take care."

Shara replaced the receiver slowly. How would Nate feel about meeting her mother and stepfather? She'd ask him tonight. She'd ask him if he'd mind spending an evening with them. It was important to her that he meet them. She didn't know why. It just was.

Going into the kitchen and lifting the lid on the crock pot, Shara stirred the beef stew. Nate was coming for supper and she hoped he was planning to stay the night. He had stayed every night this week and she loved having him with her. But she was worried about the appointment he was having with Guy Halstein. She couldn't shake off the sense of foreboding.

Danny was happily swinging in his swing when Nate appeared in the kitchen. Shara was busy slicing tomatoes and didn't hear him. He snaked his arms around her waist, nudged her ponytail aside with his chin and kissed her neck.

"Hi, beautiful. How was your day?"

She turned into his arms until she faced him. "Before I got up or after I got up?"

He grinned, his smoky eyes becoming more intense. "Getting cheeky, aren't you?"

"You like me that way." She wondered why his eyes were so serious when his words weren't.

He kissed her on the nose, then crouched down in front of Danny. "Hi, sport. I hope you didn't give your mom too much trouble today."

Shara stared at the back of Nate's thick black hair. "We've got about a half hour before his fussy spell starts. The stew's ready if you are."

He stood, evading her eyes. "I'll go change into shorts. I'll be right back."

When Nate returned to the kitchen in his cut-offs and red T-shirt, Shara's heart skipped a beat. He was so darn sexy.

"You like what you see?" he teased as she continued to stare.

She wrinkled her nose at him. "I'm trying to imagine what Danny will look like at your age."

"He'll probably have long hair and two earrings the way trends are going."

"Bite your tongue!"

"A braid?" Nate suggested.

"Nate!"

He laughed. "You'll love him anyway."

"I'll love him anyway," she agreed with a sheepish look. She dished out two plates of stew and arranged bakery-fresh rolls in a basket while Nate poured two glasses of iced tea.

He took two napkins out of the holder and placed them

beside their plates. "It smells delicious. I could get used to coming home to this."

"You want beef stew every night?" she joked as she took forks out of the silverware drawer.

"No, I want you sitting across from me as often as possible," he said quietly, his voice conveying the depth of his desire.

With more calm than she was feeling, she asked, "How was your meeting?"

Nate waited until Shara was seated, then sat down across from her. "Halstein offered me a job."

Her jaw went slack. "A job? What kind of job?"

Nate told her.

Fear gnawed at her stomach. "What answer did you give him?"

"I didn't. He gave me a month to think about it."

"I see," she said softly as her eyes lowered to her plate.

Nate picked up his fork and put it back down. "If I take it, I'll lose you, won't I?" She didn't answer. "Won't I?"

She couldn't stare at her food forever, just as she couldn't ignore the changes his job would bring. "How often would you take off on . . . assignments?"

"As often as I wanted, probably more often than I go now."

"What about the newspaper?" Her hand gripped her iced-tea glass harder than it should have. She loosened her fingers, afraid the tumbler would break.

"I could keep it and give Jerry full rein or I could sell it."

"You'd have to move to Baltimore."

"You could move with me," he returned.

That would require a commitment she didn't know if

he was willing or even capable of making. Instead of confronting him with that, she used something easier. "You have a house here."

"You haven't answered my question, Shara." His voice had lowered a register, manifesting his anxiety.

She pushed a potato across her plate, her throat tightening from just thinking about Nate leaving on an assignment as often as he wished. Why would he even want her in Baltimore? He'd never see her. Where would she and Danny fit in? Which would be more important? Them or his career?

She cut a carrot in half with her fork. "You have to make the decision. Not me."

He let out a draft of air. "You're involved. I want to know your feelings."

She felt as if she was lost in the wilderness with no survival skills and she exploded. "You *know* my feelings. They haven't changed. I don't want to be involved with someone who leaves on a whim. What will that do to Danny? What will that do to me? What happens when the assignments come in one after the other and you're gone more than you're home?"

"That won't happen."

"Are you considering the job?" she shot back.

"I'm thinking about it. It's not an opportunity I can dismiss on the spot."

She wished he would. With all her heart, she wished he could. "That means it's what you want. It means living in York isn't enough and will probably never be enough."

His eyes glinted with confused emotions. She abandoned all pretext of eating and sat back in her chair with her hands folded in her lap.

Nate's hand became a fist. "I won't lose you because of a job."

Her eyes stung. She couldn't believe she was in this position again. Nate wanted her to say she'd stand beside him no matter what he did. Her feelings told her to give him an ultimatum, to make him choose between her and the job. Logic told her an ultimatum would build a wall between them. She didn't know which way to turn.

Danny's swing had wound down and he was getting restless. She wound the mechanism again and turned back to the table. "I don't want to talk about this tonight."

"I've never seen you run from anything, but you're running from this. You're running from us."

"Aren't you?" she tossed back. "It seems to me hopping from place to place is running, too."

"Shara, we can't let this come between us."

"It's already between us. I need some time to think."

The lines around Nate's mouth were grim. "Alone?"

It was difficult to meet his eyes, but she did. "Yes."

He rose to his feet. "I'll be at home. Call me when you want to talk." He stopped in the doorway, his eyes pinning her to her chair. "While you're thinking, don't forget to feel."

Seconds later he was gone and Shara felt . . . empty.

The next afternoon, Shara's mouth dropped with surprise at the sight that met her when she answered the knock at her door. Amber was standing there in a yellow lace dress with a gardenia corsage on her shoulder. Leon was with her and sweating profusely. His lank brown hair lay across his forehead as if it were plastered there. His beard with its flecks of gray made him look as hot as he probably was.

Shara motioned them inside. "Where are you going?"

"Wrong question," Leon said, putting his arm around Amber. "Ask us where we've *been*."

Shara was puzzled. Amber was usually the ebullient one, and she was standing there shyly not saying a word. "Okay. Where have you been?"

Leon beamed. "We've been to the justice of the peace. Fifteen minutes ago, we were married."

Shara's eyes widened; her mouth rounded. When Amber held out her left hand, Shara squealed. "You did it! You actually did it! Amber. You didn't tell me. How long have you been planning this?"

The redhead looked sheepish. "Just since the weekend. We didn't invite anybody to the wedding because I was nervous and didn't know if I was going to go through with it."

"She did real good," Leon praised. "Her voice quivered and her hands were as cold as ice cream, but she made it through." He held up Amber's hand in a sign of victory. "We're married. As soon as we pack the car, we're gone for three days in the Poconos. When we get back, we'll live at Amber's till we can find a bigger place."

He looked at his new wife affectionately. "If you want a few minutes alone with Shara, I'll start loading the car."

After a slow parting kiss that turned Amber's face pink, Leon waved at Shara and left. Amber fanned her face with her hand and headed for the recliner.

"What made you change your mind?" Shara asked as she followed her friend into the living room.

Amber plopped her purse on the end table. "Taking care of Danny last weekend affected us both. Simply put, Leon gave me an ultimatum. He said if our relationship was going to stop short of marriage, he wanted out. When I thought about losing him, never having children with him, I changed my mind.''

Shara's gaze was curious. "You didn't feel coerced?"

"I did Saturday night. I felt terrifically pressured. But once I made the decision Sunday afternoon, I felt free. Free to love him more deeply. I was nervous today. But when I took those vows, I knew I was doing the best thing for both of us.''

Amber suddenly grabbed her purse. "I've been meaning to give this to you." She pulled out two pieces of paper folded into quarters and opened them. "So I didn't go out of my mind last night waiting for today's ceremony, I finished Nate's chart. I have a copy of yours, too. You two are extremely compatible.''

The two drawings looked like large pies spliced in uneven pieces with notations around the edge. Shara wasn't feeling compatible with Nate right now. She hadn't called him last night and she didn't know if she could call him tonight.

Although she was sure Amber's charts wouldn't help her, she asked, "What makes you say that?"

"His Venus is in your fifth house. That's the strongest combination you can get. You're both sensitive, interested in love, not money. His sun is also in your fifth house. That strengthens your chances even more. You're air. He's fire. So you enhance each other. You're Libra, he's Sagittarius. That's a good match on any astrologer's chart. There are some problems, though. Your moon is opposite Nate's Uranus. Nate can stimulate your imagination, but you have a tendency to remain cautious and that can cause problems. But Nate's sun is conjunct with your Jupiter. That means you'll support each other no matter what.''

"Mumbo jumbo," Shara muttered. "Nate's been offered a job in Baltimore that will put him in the field more than he is now. If you want to be helpful, tell me if he's going to take it."

Amber shook her head. "Astrologers can't predict the future, but the good ones can predict trends according to the charts."

"So what's the trend for me and Nate?" Shara's voice caught. If only a chart or an astrologer could tell her what to do.

"I could lie and tell you I didn't check it out. But I did. You're both in a period of turbulence. You have to listen to your inner voices and pay attention to your strengths. That's the way you'll find answers."

"How can I love and depend on a man who can't make a commitment?"

"Has he said he can't?"

Shara looked down at her feet. "If he takes this job, I know he can't."

"Shara, be careful. Loving him doesn't mean changing him."

"Don't you think I know that?"

Amber slid forward on the chair, her yellow pumps sturdily set on the floor. "Intellectually you might. But emotionally . . . You have to decide what you can accept and what you can't and stand by your decision. That's what Leon did with me. But I think you should consider something. If you make Nate prove too much, if you ask him to give up what he loves doing, his feelings toward you might change. You could lose something precious."

"He hasn't told me he loves me." Her voice was a whisper.

"Have you told him?"

"No. I guess I didn't realize until last night how much he means to me. But if I tell him now, I'm afraid he'll feel I'm emotionally blackmailing him. I can't do that."

Amber's gold earring swung. "You *are* in a pickle. But I know you. You'll figure it out. Just don't forget to listen to your heart as much as your head."

Essentially, Nate had said the same thing. The monitor on the coffee table pulled Shara's attention away from Amber. Danny had awakened and was cooing.

Amber smiled. "He'll be calling you in a few minutes and Leon will be calling me. The sooner we get away, the sooner we can begin our honeymoon. You'll bring in my mail?"

"You know I will."

Amber stood, and Shara hugged her. She was thankful Amber had found happiness. Now what could she do to secure her own?

After Shara fixed herself a salad for supper, she called Jenny and asked her to baby-sit. The teenager was free and said she'd be right over.

Shara drove to Nate's still not sure what she was going to say to him. She just knew she had to clear the air. Nate had given her a key to his house and when he didn't answer the bell, she checked the side window of the garage. The van was there. She let herself in the front door, knowing he was probably in the darkroom. When she went down to the basement, the darkroom door was shut.

She knocked. "Nate, it's Shara."

She heard a muffled, "Give me five minutes."

Shara leaned against the doorjamb and waited. It was

funny, but all the times she'd been in this house, she had never been inside Nate's darkroom.

When Nate opened the door, his smile was tentative. He would have stepped over the threshold, but instead Shara stepped inside. "So this is where you work."

He searched her eyes as if trying to gauge her mood. "I probably spend more time in here than I do in my living room."

There were no windows. A fan was humming, circulating the air. A table for developing and enlarging equipment sat along one wall. There were cabinets for supplies, a small sink, a work counter. Developing reels hung on a large pegboard. Boxes were lined on a shelf and were labeled "negatives."

Shara crossed the room and ran her hand over the lid on one box. "How many of these do you have?"

"Thousands." He pointed to the labels on the side with dates. "These are the most recent. The rest are in a fire-proof safe upstairs."

Shara looked at the contact sheets that were hanging on a line to dry. There were pictures of children minimally dressed, sloshing in a water-filled gutter after a thunderstorm.

"You do such a good job with faces. You ought to put together a book," she suggested, stalling before she had to say what she came to say.

"I've never thought of doing that," he said quietly. "Where's Danny?"

"Jenny's baby-sitting. She was telling me about the college life at—"

"Shara." Nate's eyes were dark gray with impatience.

She capitulated. "I know, we have to talk. I still don't want to, but I don't want this distance between us, either."

"There doesn't have to be any distance." He closed the physical gap between them.

When he reached for her, she backed away. "Not yet. I have to say a few things first."

He held up his hands, showing he wouldn't touch her. "Okay. Shoot."

She gave a rueful smile because that was exactly what she was going to do. "You have to make the decision about this job on your own despite the consequences."

His eyes lost their usual warmth. "That sounds like a threat."

Her heart lurched. She didn't want to hurt him, she didn't want to make him angry. But she had to make her position perfectly clear. "It's not a threat, it's not blackmail, it's not an ultimatum, it's reality. I can't tell you what to do. I won't tell you what to do. If I did, you'd resent me or hate me."

"I could never hate you."

"Nate, if I make you stay when you want to go, if I want you to sit in an office all day but you long to be where the action is, don't you see how you'd lose respect for yourself and me? You've got to stay because you want to stay. You have to choose with no coercion on my part. If you don't, all your life you'll wonder and you'll regret. I can't live with that any more than you can."

"What happens if I take the job?" he asked, making her face the possibility.

She sighed. She couldn't imagine living without him. But if she had to for her sake and Danny's . . . She was so confused. "I feel like Scarlett O'Hara wanting to put serious decisions off until tomorrow." She gave him a half-smile. "I don't know what to do except to take one day at a time. At least until you make your decision."

Nate couldn't still his nervous energy. He paced across the small room. Looking at a camera on one shelf, all the tools and ingredients that helped him with his craft, he said, "I make the wrong decision and you're gone. Is that what you're saying?"

"Nate, please don't push me. You're the one who wants to live in the present."

He turned toward her. "I won't push if there's hope. I won't push if you promise you'll talk to me about your feelings. I won't push if you try to understand the work I do and the way I live." He could see her torment. He could see her confusion. This time he curved his hands around her shoulders, pulled her to him, and didn't give her a chance to back away. She burrowed into his chest and held him tightly.

Halstein had given Nate a month. He would take the month to decide, to think about commitment, and Danny, and Shara, and what the future could hold if they were a family.

He leaned back and lifted her chin. Their eyes embraced. "One day at a time."

Shara loosened her hold on Nate and began to unbutton his shirt. He knew why. When they made love, there were no differences between them. No distance. No questions.

She slipped her hand in under the shirt placket and he sucked in a draft of air. "When you touch me, all hell breaks loose."

"Or all heaven?" she asked with a knowing smile.

"Sweetheart, if heaven is anything like this, I'll be good the rest of my life."

"You *are* good, Nate. And kind. And gentle. And giving."

"The last time I looked, my halo had slipped off." He

pulled up her knit top and lifted it over her head. "No angel could do what I plan on doing to you."

"You've met a few angels, have you?" she teased.

"You don't have a bra on!"

He looked so astonished she couldn't suppress a ripple of laughter. "How about that. It must mean I'm not an angel, either."

He trailed his forefinger around her breast. The nipple perked up, waiting for more attention. His eyes went back to her face. "You're a woman, Shara. A beautiful woman. I wouldn't want you to be anything else."

Shara unbuckled Nate's belt. Her hands teased over his stomach before she unfastened the hook holding the waistband around his lean hips.

His eyes twinkled with passion and deviltry. "Have you ever made love in a darkroom?"

She pushed Nate's shorts off his hips and they fell. His navy-blue briefs were already stretching in anticipation. "We won't have to worry about anyone watching us."

"Maybe I should set up the camera on delayed action. We could get some very interesting shots."

"Interesting?"

He took her upper lip between his teeth and laved it with his tongue. She began trembling and he stopped. "Hot. Very hot."

She ran her fingers around the waistband of his briefs and let her thumbs dip inside. "Sizzling."

He unsnapped her shorts. "We'd burn out the shutter."

Nate stripped off Shara's shorts and panties. She removed his briefs. She stared at his straining desire, pleased she could have that effect on him.

"You don't have to merely look. You can touch, too." His voice was husky with desire.

She stroked him slowly, moving around the velvety pouch and sliding over the thrust of his desire. When he groaned, she gave him a sultry smile. "Are you sure you don't want to move to the bedroom?"

"Are you going to do the same thing you're doing now?"

"Um hm."

"Then let's not spoil the mood."

He seduced her cheek with his thumb, trailed along her hairline down her neck. He felt Shara catch her breath as she leaned back against the counter. Her eyes were becoming greener with passion and he felt desire stampeding through him like wild horses bound for freedom.

"You are the most sensual woman I've ever known," Nate said hoarsely. "You move like a waltz, you smile like a song, you give as freely as the sun shines."

"Nate McKendrick, there's poetry in your soul," she whispered in wonder.

"Words are part of my business. It's the feelings behind the words I want you to hear."

She twined her arms around his neck. "I hear the feelings."

He ducked his head to kiss her, and she was more than ready. There was a pain inside her that only Nate could turn into pleasure. It was the pain of loving and being afraid of losing. Her hands caressed his loins, building her own anticipation.

Nate stopped the kiss so he could adore her breasts. While he taunted one with his mouth, his hand teased the other. Shara cried out his name and pressed into him.

Nate ground his hips against hers while his mouth went back to her lips. He needed her, loved her, with a ferocity that made him quake.

While Nate devoured her with his lips and tongue, his hand insinuated between them, slid over her abdomen, lingered in the dark delta between her thighs, and tested her readiness. She was hot, slick, waiting to be filled.

Shara threw her head back, her hair swishing across her shoulders. Nate caught the fragrance of her shampoo and the aroma of their scents mingling. He was driven to possess her, to keep her his for the rest of their lives. He cupped her bottom, lifted her above him, then slowly, deliciously, erotically, let her slide down his body until they joined.

"Nate," she breathed into his neck. "You make me feel so wonderful." Her long legs curled around his hips as her arms tightened around his neck.

Nate moved skillfully as his large hands guided her hips in a motion that drove him deeper into the heart of her womanhood. He felt her nails dig into his shoulders and her primal need to possess drove him on.

Shara began to quiver with passion as her thighs gripped him harder. Braced between the counter and his hard body, she was drowning, drowning in him. There was no life raft, no safety buoy. She was lost in the middle of the ocean with no shore in sight.

A whirlpool began eddying around her until she was being sucked in, whirling and whirling until her body went rigid. She cried Nate's name and almost made him lose his balance. He tilted her against the counter, moved her up and down until, a few moments later, his body shook, echoing his completion. He wasn't ready to let go of Shara, to end their fusion, but his legs were shaking. Managing to sit down on a stool, he held her as she still surrounded him.

He couldn't begin to estimate how long they sat there

in silence, still loving each other, neither one wanting to move away. Until abruptly Nate said, "Shara, I didn't think. Did you have your diaphragm in?"

"Yes."

He played with the ends of her hair. "Whew! All you need would be to get pregnant—"

"I think it might be more of a problem for you than for me."

"I'd never shirk my responsibility."

She unpasted her breasts from his chest and leaned back. "There's more to responsibility than financial aid."

He felt as if she'd slapped him. "You don't think I know that? What kind of man do you think I am?"

Shara sighed and wriggled off Nate's lap. He tried to grab her back but she eluded him and began to pick up her clothes.

He hopped to his feet and grabbed her elbows. "Answer me, Shara."

His fingertips pressed into her soft flesh, revealing the intensity of his feelings. "I'm not sure. I don't know what you want because *you* don't. I don't know what Danny and I mean to you. Are we nice to have around? Are we entertainment? Are we temporarily giving you something you need?"

Her eyes dueled with his, demanding answers he couldn't give. But he did know one thing. "I need you. Now. At this moment. Can you accept that?"

Her lower lip quivered and she stared at him. "Yes."

He decreased the pressure on her arms and soothed the flesh he had been holding tight.

She tipped her chin up. "I have a favor to ask."

"What?"

"My mother and stepfather are flying in for a weekend and I want you to meet them. Will you?"

He could see how important this was to her. Meeting parents. A band tightened around his chest. He couldn't deny her . . . and maybe he'd understand her better if he got to know them. "You set it up. I'll be there."

The tension eased from her face. He tenderly caressed her cheek. "How long is Jenny keeping Danny?"

"Another hour or so."

"Let's take a shower."

She smiled. "Together or separately?"

He rubbed his hands up and down her upper arms. "Do you have to ask?"

"You want me to scrub your back, right?" she asked as her fingers dawdled in the hair on his chest.

"Among other things."

She seemed to think about it for a while. "Could you give me a list so I know what to expect?"

His hands targeted her ribs and he began tickling. "Nate," she yelped. "Don't. I hate to be tickled."

He didn't stop the playful attack. "I have to teach you some respect for your lover."

She dropped her clothes and swatted at his hands. "Stop it!"

Her hair swished against his cheek as she squirmed, trying to get away from his hands. "You are a handful, woman."

When his arms closed around her, his fingers stopped tormenting. "A handful?" she questioned breathlessly.

He squeezed her tight. "Armful might be a better word." He gave her a hard, quick kiss. "Now about that list." He whispered all the erotic things he could do to her in the shower before he wrapped his arm around her and guided her out of the darkroom.

TEN

With a determined stride, Nate hurried toward adventure on Sunday afternoon and led Shara across a field. He was going to help her feel and taste and hear freedom. Maybe after today she'd understand the energy and force his career added to his life, he thought, as Queen Anne's lace brushed his calves.

"Won't you tell me where we're going?" she asked.

"I want to show you something."

"Nate, I like surprises. Really, I do. But can't you give me a hint?"

"Not a chance. A surprise is a surprise. No hints."

He had asked her to get a baby-sitter for this afternoon. Usually he liked having Danny with them. But today was theirs. They needed the time alone.

"Lancaster County countryside is beautiful. But we parked in the middle of nowhere! What could you want to show me out here?"

"Patience is a virtue, Shara."

"You think mine's in short supply?"

He stopped walking and hooked his arms around her, locking them at the back of her waist. "Spontaneity's not one of your strong points." Her mouth opened to protest. "You like everything organized and planned so you know exactly where you're going. I'm trying to show you that part of the fun comes in not knowing."

She closed her mouth and looked pensive. "You're right. I've had to be on top of everything for so long—"

He didn't want her thinking serious thoughts today. "You can be on top of me anytime."

She laughed and poked him in the ribs. "All right, McKendrick. Lead me to my surprise."

The clouds looked as if someone had taken a whisk and spread whipped cream across the brilliant blue sky. Green fields dotted with yellow and purple wildflowers stretched on forever. Nate felt vital and free as he swung Shara's hand back and forth between them and watched the summer breeze fan her hair along her cheek.

When they reached the top of an incline, level ground spread in acres in front of them. But something colorful sprang up forty feet from the ground. As Shara squinted against the sun, an orange, yellow, and blue hot air balloon floated against the sky.

"Nate, what is that? Is it for us?"

He gave her an unabashed grin. "We're going to take a trip."

As they walked closer, Shara asked, "Is it safe to fly in one of these?"

"We're going to forget about safe today, Shara," he responded. "We're going to see and feel." At Shara's quick glance, he reassured her. "This is a sport. The man flying this balloon is an expert. We wouldn't be here otherwise.''

"I'm . . . not sure I understand how they work.''

She was scared. He could see it on her face. But this trip was too important to let her back down. Nate stopped walking and gave her all his attention. "There's a burner that heats the air so the balloon goes up. There are two holes in the balloon, if you want to call them that. One's a valve, the other's called the rip panel. They're controlled by ropes in the basket. Troy will open them to deflate the bag as the balloon descends. I promise this will be fun, not a threat to your life. Trust me.''

She studied him for a moment and finally seemed to make up her mind. "Okay. Let's do it.''

He grinned, proud that she could overcome her fear to do something important to him. He took her hand and they scampered across the expanse of tall grass as long as a football field. After they approached the balloon, Nate introduced Shara to Troy. He was a five-foot-eight, husky blond with a smile as wide as his square jaw.

Shara ran her hand over the basket. "It's actually wicker! I thought it'd be plastic.''

"No.'' Troy patted the sides. "The woven wicker's lightweight, strong, and a good shock absorber for rough landings.''

Nate scowled. "Thanks a lot, pal. I'm trying to sell her on the trip, not make her worry about what will happen when we come down to earth!''

Troy held out a hand to Shara to help her climb into the basket. "I'm the best pilot in Pennsylvania. With the gorgeous weather we have today, we're going to soar like an eagle and land like one of its feathers.''

"He's right. Balloon pilots have to be licensed by the

Federal Aviation Administration. Troy's been piloting for nine years.''

Nate gave Shara a leg up into the basket. Once inside, she looked up. A burner was fixed to a metal platform above the basket, directly below the bag's mouth. Fuel pipes led from propane tanks to the burner.

Nate hoisted himself into the basket, his jeans scraping against the wicker.

Shara took a deep breath as if to quiet the butterflies and calm her misgivings. "I'm ready when you are."

Nate had to give her three cheers. If she was afraid, she was being a good sport. He wanted to show her that taking off into the wild blue yonder was an exhilarating experience. He had to show her what true freedom felt like.

Troy gave Nate and Shara another grin and fed more fuel to the burner. They lifted off, ascending higher and higher and higher. Shara's stomach flipped as it did when she rode the Ferris wheel. Was she crazy to do this? Is this how Nate felt every time he went off on assignment? Thrilled, scared, in this case awed at escaping earth's bonds?

Troy stayed in his corner of the basket and when Nate's arm went around her, she felt as if they were alone, suspended in midair. Should she tell him she loved him? Not with a third person present. If she did, would he feel she was trying to manipulate him? He had said he wanted her to hear the feelings behind his words. Did that mean he loved her? If so, why didn't *he* say it? For the same reason she couldn't?

Nate kissed her cheek as treetops passed beneath them. She hugged him close, trying to convey what she was feeling. Lancaster farmland had never looked so beautiful or exotic. From their bird's-eye view, barns with hex signs, tractors and combines, looked like Fisher Price toys. As they floated over a main thoroughfare, an Amish buggy traveling behind a line of cars looked odd yet quaint. Shopping malls took on the appearance of plastic boxes and they seemed removed from the beauty of earth and clouds and sky. Telephone and electric wires belonged to the boundaries of earth. The balloon and Shara and Nate belonged to something larger, a universe without limits.

Nate took his arm from around Shara. She watched curiously as he pulled a carafe of wine and two plastic glasses from a bag. When she looked over at Troy, Nate said, "He can't have any. He's driving."

He poured the wine and offered Shara a half-filled glass. Amusement lurked in his eyes. "We might hit a wind pocket." After clicking his glass against hers, he took a sip. So did she. As the wind ruffled their hair, Nate's lips slid over hers. The wine wasn't as potent as the kiss. Their tongues mated, danced in loving play, entwined, and when they wanted much more, retreated.

Shara whispered into Nate's neck, "Imagine making love up here."

He tipped her chin up. "Are you getting adventurous?"

"Not enough to have a third person watching," she jibed.

Nate laughed—a deep rich sound that flew around Shara and warmed her. When the basket tilted slightly and Shara fell into him, he caught her tight against his body. "Maybe we could find a way to simulate this. I could buy a waterbed."

She could feel his heart beating under his yellow polo shirt. "We could paint clouds on the ceiling."

He wiggled his brows. "I'd rather have mirrors." He snuck a look at Troy who was pretending to be involved in flying the balloon, but the pilot's expression said he'd heard. "I think we're entertaining our pilot."

She winked. "Maybe we should take this show on the road."

"Amber could be our manager. I bet she'd be a great promoter."

"Instigator's more likely. She'd only let us perform when the stars were lined up right. She did your astrological chart and showed it to me."

He looked amused. "Anything I should know?"

"She says we're compatible."

He smoothed his hand down Shara's hair as if he loved to touch it. "I don't need a chart to tell me that. Anything else?"

Shara didn't feel comfortable telling him the rest of Amber's analysis. It certainly wasn't anything concrete. They both knew they were going through a period of turbulence. "Nothing important. You don't believe in that stuff, do you?"

He shrugged. "I wouldn't consult my horoscope before stepping out the door everyday, but I don't believe we can separate ourselves from life around us. That includes the moon and sun and stars." He grinned. "Don't you get a little restless when the moon is full?"

"Maybe. We'll have to check the calendar and plan something active next full moon."

Nate's expression clearly stated what that would be. Shara sipped the last of her wine and put the glass back in the bag.

"There's more," he offered.

She shook her head. "I don't need it. Not while we're up here. This is enough of a high for anyone. No pun intended."

During the rest of the flight, Shara and Nate pulled Troy into conversation. Among other things, Shara discovered he attended the National Hot Air Balloon Championships in Iowa every year. With each mile she became more and more relaxed, sure the balloon was as safe as riding in a car.

After a two-hour ride, Shara began recognizing landmarks and realized they'd soon be above the field where they'd started. Troy was fueling the burner less and less. He pulled the rope and opened the rip panel. The landing was slightly bumpy, but, according to Nate, gentle. Nate helped Shara out of the basket and they said good-bye to Troy.

Shara felt sad. The free feeling the soaring had given her was special and one she wouldn't soon forget. She was sorry it was over.

As she ambled beside Nate, he noted, "You're awfully quiet."

She hooked her arm through his. "Just thinking about the ride. It was great. I don't know how to thank you."

"There are many ways," he said slyly.

She motioned to the surrounding countryside. "I could pick you wildflowers."

"That would be nice," he said with a straight face.

She caught her bottom lip between her teeth to keep from smiling. As seriously as she could, she surmised, "But not exactly what you had in mind."

"Not exactly," he agreed.

"I could cook you dinner," she proposed.

"That would be nice, too."

"But I'm still not reading your mind."

"Nope."

She put her finger to her cheek. "I could buy mirrors for your ceiling."

"*Now* you're getting closer."

"Black silk sleeping trunks?" She stole a glance at him.

"What about *you* in black silk in the middle of my bed?"

She opened her eyes wide and fluttered her lashes. "Why, Mr. McKendrick. What kind of proper lady thanks a man like that?"

"*My* kind of lady. And you're definitely my kind of lady."

His eyes simmered with passion she could increase to a full-blown boil with a look, a touch, or a kiss. She reached up and stroked the side of his jaw. "I had a lovely time."

"I wasn't too sure if you would when you first climbed in the basket. But I knew if you gave it a chance . . . I wanted you to feel the excitement and thrill I feel every time I take an assignment."

"This was an experiment to see how I'd react?"

"No." He was unruffled by her sharp tone. "I wanted to share some of the adventure and . . . freedom."

His smile disarmed her flare of temper. "It could have backfired. I could have hated it."

He shook his head. "I know you better than that. No way could you hate soaring through heaven."

"I could have gotten seasick," she persisted.

"Nope." He took her arm again to walk back to the van. "I watched you jump off the high dive when we went swimming. Nobody who can do that gets seasick."

The long grass prickled her ankles. "You're pretty sure of yourself."

He wasn't a bit repentant. "Just trying out a few theories."

She glanced at him out of the corner of her eye. "I'm afraid to ask what you have planned next."

"We could try an African safari. I've always wanted to do some wildlife photography."

"Start with cows," she countered dryly. "It'll be safer."

"You don't know the same cows I do. When my uncle gave me my first camera, he said, 'Start out easy. Photograph what's in your own backyard.' He had a farm and *his* backyard looked more interesting than mine. I started with the kittens. They scampered around too quickly. The horses were fairly cooperative. So I ventured into the field with the cows. They must have thought I was the paparazzi. The grande dame of the herd took one whiff of me and decided chasing me was more fun than chewing on grass. When she took off, two others followed. I never ran so fast in my life. Tore my britches leaping over the fence."

Shara laughed at the picture he painted.

He shook her arm. "It was *not* funny. I was scared out of my wits. My mother wasn't too thrilled about my pants."

"Did you get any pictures?"

"Oh, sure. While I was running. I was afraid the cow would eat my camera."

Shara broke out in a fresh batch of giggles. "I guess you went back to photographing horses."

"Actually, I switched to girls."

"It was great having *them* chase you."

"Not bad."

She jabbed him in the ribs.

"You can chase me any time you want," he added. "I'll even let you catch me."

"Don't cut me any breaks," she warned, deciding exactly what she was going to do so he didn't feel so superior. She took a minute to prepare, then sprinted ahead of him and shouted, "Come on, McKendrick. Let's see your stuff. We'll see who catches who."

"Whom," he corrected as he raced after her.

Shara's sneakers pounded the ground, her arms swung, and her hair blew behind her. She was smaller and more streamlined than Nate, but her size wasn't enough to give her an edge. Nate's long legs easily brought him to her side.

He tagged her and ordered, "Stop. You should know you can't get away from me."

But she didn't stop. She escaped his hand and kept running. Calling over her shoulder, she yelled, "I'm not caught until I'm caught!"

He shook his head and bounded after her. "You're making this rough on yourself. You could give in and save your energy."

"Never," she flung back.

Nate jogged up to her, curled his arm around her waist, and tumbled her to the long grass. He braced her fall and she lay sprawled on top of him. Squirming, she tried to roll away, but he reversed their positions and pinned her wrists above her head. "You're more temperamental than that herd of cows."

She struggled to release her hands. "Herd? You said there were three cows! You never told me you were prone to tall tales."

He wiggled his hips against hers. "Let's just say I'm prone."

She squirmed again, trying to break his hold, and muttered, "I should have learned self-defense."

Her struggling was making their position more erotic. He knew she could feel the strength of his desire. "Self-defense is only useful when used against someone who has ill intent toward you."

"Should I ask what your intentions are?" she bantered, lying still because she wasn't in the mood any longer to escape.

He loosened his hold on her wrists, lowered himself to his elbows, and encouraged her breasts to brush his chest. "My intentions are very honorable. And fun."

"Nate!" she gasped. "You aren't seriously thinking about . . ."

His brows arched seductively. "The van's half a mile away. Troy's going off in the other direction. There's nobody around for miles."

Grass was tickling her ear. "But what if—?"

"What if we pretend no one else exists? It's you, me, sun, and sky."

She'd never done anything so impulsive, so completely abandoned. Did she dare? His eyes said he was waiting for her answer. "Convince me," she whispered as if she were afraid someone would hear.

"Gladly," he breathed.

As the smell of warm earth, summer wind, green grass, and Nate drugged her, she wondered if she had won the race, if he had caught her, or if she had caught him. His lips touched hers and she didn't care. They were together. That was all that mattered.

When Nate opened Jerry's office door Monday morning, he heard the click-clacking of a keyboard's keys. Jerry's concentration was focused on the computer screen.

Nate picked up a pile of newspapers on a blue vinyl

chair and plunked them on the floor. "Is this the editorial on the new school?"

Jerry didn't turn away from the screen. "Sure is. Man, what a furor! All those letters about using the old buildings instead of building a new one. The superintendent's meeting with the city council tonight. I might try and get into the meeting."

Nate locked his hands at the back of his neck and stretched. "You set up the debate by airing both sides."

Jerry finished the paragraph he was typing and jabbed the return. "Isn't that what we're supposed to do? Inform and make people question and think?"

Loosening his tie, Nate replied, "That's what I like about this business."

Jerry turned away from the screen to face Nate. "Are you going to stay in it?"

"Yes. No matter what I decide about Halstein's offer, I'm going to keep the paper. That is, if you decide to run it for me."

Jerry picked up a pen on his desk and tapped the end on the blotter. "It won't be the same if you're not here."

Nate stood up and examined the pop art poster Jerry had hung on his wall. "I trust you. I'd only be a phone call away."

"You're going to take it."

"I didn't say that," Nate denied as he picked up a baseball signed by Mickey Mantle that was sitting on the file cabinet. Yesterday had been a success beyond his wildest dreams. Making love to Shara in the middle of a meadow had to be the Garden of Eden revisited. But reality had set in soon enough.

When they'd returned to Shara's townhouse, Danny's nose was running. She thought he might be beginning the teething process. Nate had wanted to stay the night, but Shara had insisted since he had to go to work the next day that he go home. She was afraid neither of them would get much sleep if he stayed. He often sensed she felt Danny had to be good for Nate to love him. That just wasn't so. Maybe he should talk to her about that tonight.

When Nate turned around, Jerry was studying him thoughtfully. "What's holding you back from accepting Halstein's offer?"

"Not just Shara, if that's what you're thinking. I like being my own boss. I don't like to have to explain my comings and goings."

"He'd give you latitude."

Nate leaned against the cabinet. "Maybe. Or maybe he'd become more demanding over time. He won't consider what's best for my life. He'll only consider what's good for the magazine and what will make money. Profit's his bottom line. I know Halstein well enough to know that."

"Profit is why he wants you." Jerry stayed Nate's protest with, "He knows he'll get his money's worth. Then again, if Shara moves with you and you put her before your job, Halstein's not going to like it. And then there's the kid."

"What do you mean?"

"A few years down the line there will be PTA meetings, Little League. Things that could get in your way if Shara expects you to be involved."

"I have a few years before I have to worry about the PTA."

"Mmm." After a meaningful pause, Jerry asked, "Is she prepared to move to Baltimore?"

"Jerry, I told you—"

"Yeah. You don't know if you're taking the job," he finished for Nate, repeating something he didn't seem to believe. Jerry blew out a heavy sigh. "I don't think you understand women."

"And you're going to explain them to me?" Nate asked with a combination of amusement and irritation. "You're not even married."

Jerry thumped his hand on the desk. "You're darn right. You wanna know why?"

"You're going to tell me whether I want to know or not."

"Women need two things. They need to be told and shown they're loved." Jerry warmed to the subject he had obviously examined carefully. "The telling's not so hard. The showing? That's something else. We're not just talking flowers and candy here. We're talking real proof."

At the gleam in Nate's eyes, Jerry admonished, "Not that, either. The bedroom's separate from what I'm talking about. It's like they set up tests. I'll bet you the next daily double I win that Shara's thinking to herself, If he loves me, he won't take that job."

Nate didn't like the tack Jerry was taking. "She said it was my decision."

Jerry snorted. "Oh, it's your decision, all right, but you better make the right one."

That was the worry gnawing at Nate. He didn't want to lose her.

His time deliberating seemed to prove Jerry's point. Nate's editor-in-chief said, "You've got to remember where she's coming from. She has a son, Nate. She doesn't want her child to get attached to you—not if there's a chance you won't stay together. Can you blame her for protecting herself and her son? Nothing's as fierce as a mother's love. Nothing.''

At Nate's frustrated scowl Jerry asked, "You want to take the safe route? Forget about the job. Be happy with what you've got. Maybe even get married and cut back on the miles you travel. The job with Halstein is a gamble. If you want to take the risk, you can go for double or nothing. But remember, you could wind up with nothing.''

Had Jerry wound up with nothing? Is that why he could see the situation so clearly? Nate couldn't see it clearly. Not yet. He hoped he would soon.

Putting another bottle in the microwave, Shara cast a worried glance at Danny. He was screaming at the top of his lungs. Shara checked the clock—four P.M. Nate had told her he'd pick up Chinese on the way to her place. At this rate he'd want to drop it off and leave. She'd had a rough night and a rougher day. Danny's stuffy nose had kept him awake most of the night. Her, too.

When the microwave beeped, Shara took out the bottle and shook it. She picked up Danny. He was as red as a beet, squirming and wiggling, and Shara was scared. He wouldn't drink. He had eaten practically nothing all day. This was different from him being stuffy and uncomfortable. He was in pain. She'd always thought a baby's immunity lasted the first six months. Apparently she'd been wrong.

When no amount of cuddling or crooning would help, Shara laid Danny in his bassinet and reached for the phone. Danny's pediatrician didn't have office hours on Thursdays, but she knew she could reach his answering service. When she did, she gave them the pertinent information they needed. The woman at the other end of the line said the doctor would call back.

Shara wanted to call Nate. He was a calming influence, always knowing what to say to make her feel better. But maybe he wouldn't want to help this time. A sick baby wasn't as easy to calm as a hot one, or a hungry one, or a wet one.

She paced and tried to soothe Danny until the phone rang. Rushing to it, she picked it up on the first ring. After again describing Danny's symptoms, Dr. Lassiter directed her to meet him at the emergency room at the hospital.

Shara then put in a call to Nate's office. At least she could tell him where she'd be, even if he decided not to come. After waiting a minute that seemed more like a year, her call was transferred to Jerry.

"Hi, Shara," he greeted cheerfully. "What can I do for you?"

"I need to talk to Nate. Is he with you?"

"He was. He left about ten minutes ago. He had an appointment downtown."

"Can you tell me where I can reach him? I wouldn't normally do this, but it's an emergency and—"

"Shara, I'm sorry. He said something about his accountant. But it's his personal accountant, not the one the paper uses and I don't know his name. I'm really sorry. Can I do anything to help?"

"No. No, there's nothing you can do. I'll leave a note here, but if he would come back to the paper or call in, would you tell him I'm at the emergency room?"

"Are you sure I can't help?"

"I'm sure. I have to get going. Thanks, Jerry."

Shara hung up, left a note for Nate on the refrigerator,

hurriedly stuffed the diaper bag, picked up Danny, and headed for the hospital wishing Nate was beside her. At least she knew she could contact him eventually. He was in the same town. But what if this was serious? What if Nate had been away on assignment where she couldn't reach him? *Stop it, Shara. That sort of thinking won't get you anywhere.*

She stepped on the gas and her car zoomed toward the hospital.

ELEVEN

The emergency room was full of people. Some appeared to be waiting for relatives, four or five needed treatment themselves. Danny's crying created a continual disturbance. The nurse at the desk explained to Shara that Dr. Lassiter had been delayed by an emergency but he would examine Danny as soon as he could.

Filling out insurance information while trying to console a crying child could wear down the patience of Job. Shara felt like screaming herself until she saw Nate come striding toward her. The worry on his face mirrored her own. A rush of relief streamed through her now that Nate was with her.

He took Danny from her and held the baby at his shoulder. "Do you know anything yet?"

"No, I just got here. But I have to get this form filled out and Danny's yelling—"

Nate rested his free hand on the back of her neck. "I'll walk him around the room while you do what you have to."

Her eyes held his. "Thank you for being here."

His long fingers brushed along her neck. "No thanks necessary." He moved away, patting Danny's behind.

After Shara handed in the forms, the nurse led Nate, Shara, and Danny to an examining room. Nate kept walking back and forth attempting to quiet Danny while Shara crossed her legs and swung her foot restively.

"How long has he been like this?"

Shara wiped her cold, clammy hands on her yellow slacks. Danny looked so small against Nate's shoulder. "He didn't sleep much last night because he was stuffy. When I fed him at seven, he didn't drink much and he wouldn't go back to sleep. He didn't sleep all morning, and around noon, he started crying. By four it became nonstop. I didn't know what to do for him. Nothing helped. I feel helpless."

Nate laid Danny on the examining table and unfastened his diaper. "He's not acting like he does when he has colic. He's not pulling his legs up. Do you think it's more than a cold?"

Her nurse's training hadn't prepared her for her own child's illness. "I'm not sure. Nate, if anything happens to him . . ."

Nate held on to Danny with one hand and reached out to Shara with the other. Their fingers interlocked.

They were still holding hands when the door opened and Dr. Lassiter stepped in. He was in his fifties and had white hair and twinkling blue eyes. The older man patted Shara's arm, then extended his hand to Nate. As busy as he was, he didn't seem hurried.

As he took Nate's position with Danny at the examining table, Nate stepped back and put his hand on Shara's shoulder.

The doctor unsnapped Danny's nightshirt, probed his stomach and groin, used his stethoscope, a tongue depressor, and the otoscope and said more to himself than to anyone, "I thought so. This young man has an ear infection in his left ear. We can fix him up with Tylenol and an antibiotic and he'll be as good as the day he was born in less than a week. I have some samples that will get you through the night. You can have the prescription filled tomorrow."

Shara came to her feet and stood next to her son. "He won't eat."

"After we get the Tylenol in him and two or three doses of the antibiotic, the pain will subside." Dr. Lassiter took the stethoscope from around his neck and stuffed it in the pocket of his jacket. "Don't push the formula unless he wants it. Try to keep him drinking water. I'll give him an injection to start the antibiotic working faster. You can run a room humidifier to help him breathe easier. Most drugstores sell them. Do you have any questions?"

"Is this serious?" Shara's voice cracked. "What's the likelihood the infection could spread?"

"We caught it in time. I want him on the antibiotic for seven days, but you can stop the Tylenol when he seems comfortable. You'll know. The cold will run its course. This isn't common in a fellow his age, but it happens."

Dr. Lassiter prepared an injection. Danny howled louder when it pricked him. Tears came to the surface in Shara's eyes.

"When you're ready to leave, stop at the desk and pick up the samples and prescription," the doctor said. "I don't think I'll need to see him again. But don't hesitate to call me if there's a problem."

Shara was already touching Danny, rubbing his arm, trying to convey love and comfort. "He's so little. He doesn't understand what's happening. I wish I could explain it to him."

"You're doing that now. He'll respond to your touch and the love you give him when caring for him."

Nate spoke for the first time. "Shara's good at that."

She looked at him tenderly. "So are you."

Dr. Lassiter patted Shara's hand and shook Nate's again. "It was good to meet you, Mr. Nolan."

Words formed on Shara's lips, but none of them seemed right. The doctor was gone before she even considered explaining. Nate's expression was inscrutable.

Shara quickly rediapered Danny and snapped his night-shirt. Picking him up, she held him to her breast and crooned softly. His strenuous crying had subsided to a whimper. Nate picked up the diaper bag and followed Shara to the waiting room.

At the desk he asked Shara, "Do you want me to take Danny?"

"No. I'd like to keep him with me. Nate, you don't have to come over. I'll probably be up with him all night."

She was surprised by the anger in Nate's eyes that matched his scowl when he said tersely, "I'll get the pre-scriptions filled. Do you have a humidifier?"

"No, but—"

"I'll get one of them, too, and get to your place as soon as I can." He waited for the prescription and left without another word to Shara.

When Nate arrived at Shara's townhouse an hour later, she wasn't downstairs. He carried the medicine upstairs with the boxed humidifier.

Shara was sitting in the wooden rocking chair beside Danny's crib, pushing with her toes, cuddling the baby in her arms and humming. Nate stared, thinking she had never looked more lovely. It was impossible to separate Shara the mother from Shara the woman. She was complex, had so many facets. Yet she was . . . organic, not fake in any way, sincere and honest. She didn't pretend. And sometimes she made him damn angry.

He stood watching her until she looked up. "He looks like he can't keep his eyes open."

She nodded. "I know. I should put him in the crib, but I wanted to hold him."

Nate understood. He unpacked the humidifier and followed the directions to fill it. Positioning it on the dresser, he said, "I'll be downstairs. Don't hurry. There's chicken lo mein in the refrigerator for later." As she was about to open her mouth, he said gruffly, "And *don't* thank me."

Nate sank down on the sofa with the evening newspaper. His newspaper. He paged through it proudly. Would he feel as proud if he wasn't there to supervise?

Fifteen minutes later, Shara came down the steps and sat next to Nate. Pulling the tortoiseshell clip from her ponytail, she ran her hands through her hair. "He's sleeping. He drank some water. Thanks for . . ." She stopped, remembering his admonition but looking unsure as to why he'd given it.

Nate knew she'd had a rough day. He didn't want to make it any rougher. But they had to discuss . . .

The telephone rang, and he was relieved. "I'll get it," he said and crossed to the gossip bench. The caller was Jerry. He told Nate Shara had called the newspaper and he wanted to know if she was okay. Nate explained the situation.

When he hung up the phone, he was puzzled.

She raised her brows in question.

Sitting on the sofa, he leaned forward, his hands capping his knees. "Jerry said you called me at the office. Why?"

"Why? Because I wanted to tell you about Danny. I hoped you'd come to the hospital."

He was totally baffled. "Then why did you say I didn't have to come back here? Why do you thank me as if I'm a stranger doing something nice?"

"Because you do nice things and Mrs. Pennington raised me to be polite so I say thank you and . . ." What he had just said registered and she pounced indignantly. "I don't treat you like a stranger and you know it. A stranger! Nate, what's gotten into you?"

He hesitated before answering. "I don't want to be an outsider, Shara. I want to be involved in your life and Danny's. I want you to depend on me."

He laid out exactly what he saw and felt. "You never ask for help. I feel as if I've pushed my way into your life, and because you don't have a choice, you accept my help. I want you to ask; I want you to take as freely as you give."

Shara dropped her eyes. "I'm protecting myself, Nate."

The fans of lines around his eyes crinkled like the creases on his brow. "Against me?"

"Yes, and against myself." She tried to explain. "Do you realize how easy it would be to use your shoulders? To forget I have to be self-reliant?"

"Self-reliance is fine to a degree. But everyone needs help sometime."

Shara stood and crossed to the bowed window that overlooked the street. She stared into the dark night. "My mother had me when she was nineteen. My biological father decided marriage wasn't in the cards. A wife and child would slow him down. After I was born, my mother was alone, scared, barely making ends meet. She married the first man who could take care of her needs.''

"That's not uncommon. She probably thought of you as much as herself. Shara, people *need* other people."

It seemed the window became a crystal ball for Shara, reflecting the past instead of the future. "And what happens when you need and no one's there to fill that need? Then what, Nate?"

His voice was soothing and low. "Tell me when you needed, Shara. Tell me."

He saw the tenseness in her shoulders, the rigid hold of her head. Just as he thought she wasn't going to confide in him, the words came barreling out. "I needed my stepfather. But he didn't want a daughter. I learned that young. Mom's a beautiful woman. Chet's life revolved around them as a couple. She always felt so grateful to him, so afraid he'd desert her, too, that she's always done everything he wants.

"If a parents' day at school coincided with a business engagement, there was no contest. She didn't come to see me, she went with him. He sent me to boarding school to get me out of his hair, to reduce my demands on Mom's time. She couldn't stand up to him. I learned early on to take care of myself."

Nate felt a seething anger at Shara's parents. He saw a lonely child, searching for someone to care about her. "It shouldn't be like that."

"It was. In college, I concentrated on my studies. When I was in the Peace Corps, I taught the self-reliance I'd learned. When I married Jim, I thought finally I had someone of my own to love. I wanted to depend on him. But he was never there."

Her shoulders sagged. Nate shoved himself up and went to stand behind her. She was looking out, not at him. He put his arms around her and pulled her back against his chest and held her that way for a long time. "I'm here, Shara."

Finally she said softly, "I'm sorry Dr. Lassiter called you Mr. Nolan. I didn't know what to say."

"It was an honest mistake. Harder to explain than to let sit."

Sounds from the monitor caught Shara's attention. Danny was crying. She tried to step away from Nate. He gave her a tight squeeze. "You sit. I'll take care of him. Better yet, go warm up the Chinese. I bet you haven't eaten all day, have you?"

"No."

He kissed her forehead.

"It might take you a while to get him quiet—"

"Shara, I'll take care of him."

She gave him a weak smile and he went to answer the summons.

Now Nate knew what Shara had been going through all day. No position satisfied Danny, no amount of crooning and rocking could console him. It was a matter of waiting for the medicine to work. The night was going to be long and he wanted to alleviate the burden on Shara. Two people could cope better than one.

When he returned to the living room, he found Shara sleeping, her body curled into a corner of the sofa. He understood her better now, her need to have a "normal" family, a stable home for Danny. But understanding didn't make Nate's decision any easier. What was he waiting for? A sign? Maybe.

As he gathered Shara into his arms, she mumbled something but settled her head on his shoulder and wound her arms around his neck. In no time he'd carried her upstairs and laid her on the bed. If he undressed her, he might wake her. Besides, he'd want to touch her and she needed the sleep more.

An hour later, Nate was propped against the headboard reading *Newsweek*. Shara turned over and threw her arm across his lap. The feel of his thighs under his robe must have startled her because her eyes flew open. "What are you doing here?"

"Waiting for you to wake up."

"What if I'd slept all night?"

"You wouldn't. As soon as Danny cried, you'd be up and running."

"You're going to stay?"

He reached out and brushed her hair behind her ear. "I'm going to stay. I called Jerry because I'm staying with you tomorrow, too. And the day after, if you and Danny need me."

Her eyes grew wide and shiny. "You want to do this?"

"Yes."

"It scares me to depend on you," she murmured.

He slid down next to her and pulled her close. "I know. We'll work on that."

She buried her nose in his chest, and after a lull mumbled, "Danny's cold is my fault."

"How so?"

"I shouldn't have taken him to the day-care center. All those kids, the germs—"

"I won't argue with you because we don't know what caused it. But I do know you can't put him in a bubble and protect him forever."

She was pensive. "I guess you're right."

"I *know* I'm right."

She tweaked his nose. "Modest, aren't we?"

"More hungry than anything. Do you want to sleep or eat?"

She slipped her hand under the lapel of his robe. "Are they my only two choices?"

Her touch charged him. He'd been ready to make love with her simply from lying next to her. "Danny could wake up any minute."

Her hand skimmed over his chest and ventured south. "Then we'd better get started."

As Nate kissed her, he realized Shara had become necessary, vital, important, indispensable to his life. So what was he going to do?

Thursday afternoon, Nate sorted through the negatives scattered across his desk, thinking this was a far cry from what he'd been doing yesterday at this time. He'd stayed home with Shara Tuesday and Wednesday. Finally last night Danny had slept straight through and they both felt rested. Helping her do laundry, make meals, take care of Danny had formed another bond between them.

Today, Shara was busy getting the townhouse ready for her mother and stepfather's visit. She tried not to seem excited. She tried to act as if she didn't care. But she did. He was praying this visit would go well.

When the phone buzzed, Nate picked up the receiver mechanically. "McKendrick here."

"I've got something for you. Something that could be big."

"Halstein, is that you?" Nate asked.

"It sure as hell is. Are you going to take the job I offered?"

Nate didn't have to check his calendar. "I still have two weeks."

"Going to take it down to the wire, huh? Okay, that's the deal. But I've got something that might make you decide sooner. You take this for me, and if you want the other job, you can set your own salary without a quibble from me."

He had whetted Nate's curiosity. If Halstein was willing to promise that . . . "What's up?"

There was excitement in the publisher's voice. "It's what's coming down. Have you been listening to the national weather reports?"

"No."

"Where have you been, man?"

"I had better things to do than watch the eleven o'clock news." Nate thought about the hours spent walking Danny and holding Shara.

"Well, you'd better start watching and listening. I sent a package up to you by Purolator. You should get it in about an hour. Study it carefully."

Halstein seemed sure Nate would accept the assignment. "Guy, will you tell me what I'm supposed to be studying?"

"A hurricane. A big one. Advisories are being issued every six hours telling where the storm is located, how intense it is, and where it's moving. The first charting was near the Cape Verde Islands. She's east of the Bahamas with a barometer pressure of 27.26 inches. That's ominous. There hasn't been this much media attention since Gloria in '85. The National Weather Service has dispatched reconnaissance aircraft to look at the hurricane's interior. Experts are poring over satellite photographs and radar data. The consensus is, it's a category four hurricane. She's erratic. But they think she'll hit at South Carolina, possibly Hilton Head. Do you realize what that could mean to that resort? What a story!''

''What do you want from me?'' Nate asked, not sure how he was involved, but feeling an excitement building in his gut.

''A hurricane can be as fickle as a woman. But this one looks like it could sink a navy. I want you there. I want you wherever it hits land. If anybody can nail it down, you can.''

A hurricane was a powerful force man couldn't yet control. That's what made it glorious, destructive, and a challenge. ''What's her name?''

''Gina.''

''What if she doesn't land at Hilton Head?''

''I remember Hazel in '54. I was just starting in this business. She swept over South Carolina's beaches with winds up to 150 mph. Damage along those beaches was sixty-one million dollars. She flattened business areas and homes, destroyed fishing piers from Myrtle Beach to Cedar Island. But because of radio and warning systems only nineteen people were killed in that area. Gina's going to hit and when she does, I want you there.''

Part of Nate resented Halstein's certainty he'd go to Hilton Head. ''She could fizzle out.''

''I guess you don't remember Diane in '55.'' Halstein slipped back into another reminiscence. ''Meteorologists said she diminished to a wind disturbance and the hurricane warnings were discontinued. Yet she caused some of the most dangerous floods on record. I have a gut feeling about this one, McKendrick. We'll watch the bulletins and listen to the best prediction. This could be bigger than Hugo. Hell, bigger than the San Francisco earthquake.''

"You're presuming I'll go," Nate said coolly, not liking being taken for granted.

"Look, McKendrick. I want pictures and a report that gives an intense and immediate physical description of this baby coming in. All we usually get are vague words like 'beyond belief.' I want it in pictures and words. I want my readers to see it and feel it."

A surge of adrenaline rushed through Nate. "How can I manage that without it hitting me?"

"I have connections with the TV news crews down there. They have access to the pertinent information. You can work with them."

"You want me to fly down now?" Nate automatically scanned his appointments for the next day.

"No. I want you to study this phenomenon. That's the only way you'll know what you can get and when. The barometric pressure drops about twelve hours before the arrival of the storm center. When I get the word from the coast, I'll have somebody fly you down. You get what you can before evacuation begins. Go where you have to. Get photos from the shelter. What I want you to study is the eye of the hurricane. When you read about it, you'll understand what I mean. Will you take it?"

He was tempted by the challenge of a great natural force. He knew the tracking systems used now were excellent and, if anything, there would be overkill, not underkill. If he stuck with the people who knew what they were doing, he might get the most sensational story of the year. A story no one else could get. Adrenaline rushed faster and he felt the age-old excitement of man trying to capture the elements.

He made the decision. "I'll go. Keep me posted on any changes. When are they calculating she'll come in?"

"With the wind currents they've measured and the speed marked, they're saying forty-eight hours. I don't want you to go until they're more sure where she'll land. I want you at the best vantage point."

Nate nodded his agreement. "Makes sense. I want pictures of more than a rainstorm."

"You'll get them. I know you will. I'll call you if anything changes."

Nate gave Halstein Shara's number in case he wasn't at home. Hanging up the receiver, he suddenly remembered Shara's mother and stepfather. Shara would just have to understand. A hurricane couldn't wait.

TWELVE

Shara was dusting the living room and Danny was sitting in his stroller watching her when Nate let himself into the townhouse. He came up behind Shara, tugged on her ponytail and gave her a lingering, sweet kiss, wishing he could take her to bed rather than reveal his plans. He'd spent the afternoon reading and studying hurricanes, and he felt he had a handle on them. But explaining them to Shara was another story.

Before Shara could comment on the intensity of the kiss, he went over to Danny and tickled his knee. "He's getting to be a big kid. With those legs, he'll be great in football."

"Not if I can help it," Shara concluded in a mother-knows-best tone.

"You're not going to curb his athletic tendencies, are you?"

Her eyes flashed green sparks of protectiveness. "No, but I'm going to channel them. Tennis is much safer."

At Nate's raised brows, she reasoned, "Tennis players need great legs. Look at Pat Cash."

"Tennis players get tennis elbow," Nate said dryly.

"And football players get smashed. He doesn't need a broken nose or a fractured leg to prove he's macho." Her lips pursed together as if she wouldn't budge on the issue now or ever.

He shouldn't be arguing with her, not when he was going to drop a bomb in her lap. But something drove him on. "Macho's not so bad. It's gotten a bad rap. If a man's not a little macho, he doesn't feel like a man."

"Is that why you're . . . adventurous? It makes you feel macho?" Her chin lifted, telling him she wanted the truth.

"No. That's not it at all. I do what I do because I love to do it."

"You've decided to take the job," she said in a stunned whisper.

"No. Not yet. But we do have to talk. Halstein called today."

The tension in her body quivered in her voice. "What does he want you to do?"

"Photograph a hurricane."

"When?"

He hesitated. "Maybe tomorrow." He reached for her hand, his grip strong and sure.

She pulled away with more force than he expected and he wished he had taken her in his arms instead. "My mother's coming Saturday. You promised you'd be here!"

Nate took a bolstering breath to lighten the constriction in his chest. He didn't like what he saw in her eyes. It looked like betrayal. "I still might be. The hurricane could stall." Maybe if he explained some of the details, assured her this would be a short trip . . . "It might hit Hilton Head. We'll know more in a few hours."

The current that usually flowed between them had been broken. He was afraid if he reached out to touch her she'd cringe. He couldn't bear that. So he pulled a piece of paper out of his back pocket to give his fingers something to do rather than stroking her cheek. Opening it up and spreading it out, he explained, "This is a tracking chart."

Shara slammed her open hand down on the paper. "I don't care about charts. I want the bottom line. When will you be leaving and how long will you be gone?"

He cut his explanation down to the basics. "Six to twelve hours before the hurricane lands, Halstein wants me there. I'll get interviews, warning signs, anything pertinent. If and when evacuation orders are issued, I'll move out with the TV crew. I'll hole up somewhere where I can get pictures out a window."

"Windows are boarded up during hurricanes," she said caustically, obviously upset with the whole scenario.

"I'll drill a hole in the wall," he returned calmly.

"That seems a little tame for you. What else is involved?"

She knew him too well. If he could only touch her. But when he took a step closer, she stepped back. "There's a brief period, twenty minutes to half an hour, when the eye of the hurricane passes over. Everything's quiet. No wind. No rain. Silence. The sun comes out. That's what I want to get. It's going to be the focus of the piece." He took her hand firmly, not giving her the chance to back away, and pulled her down onto the sofa beside him.

Shara stared down at their hands. When she looked up, he saw the desire that was always there the moment they touched. At least she wasn't pushing him away.

Her fingers curled under his. "What happens if the hurricane moves in before it's expected? What happens if you have fifteen minutes instead of twenty or thirty?"

He wished he knew what to say to reassure her. "That won't happen. The technology's too good. And I know my limits."

Their discussion was interrupted by the jangling of the phone. Shara's gaze zigzagged from the gossip bench to Nate. He went to answer it.

Shara couldn't hear the conversation, only the low rumble of Nate's voice. There was a cold spreading through her, a cold that spoke of rejection and desertion and betrayal. She hated the feeling. Some part of her had expected this to happen. Nate's career was a barrier, a mountain that was too big to get around.

When Nate returned to her, she looked at him with sad eyes. "Are you leaving?"

"Not yet." He mowed his fingers through his hair and sat down on the couch next to her. "It's stalled and they don't know what it's going to do next."

"So much for computers and satellites. And the idea that I could depend on you," she added bitterly.

He grasped her by the shoulders and made her look directly into his eyes. "Shara—"

She thumped her right hand against his chest for emphasis, ignoring the hardness she loved to touch, ignoring the heat that doubled when their skin came into contact, ignoring the love she felt. "Depend isn't a sometimes thing. Either I can or I can't. And it looks like I can't."

She saw the yearning on Nate's face, the need to make her understand as he asked, "Why do you insist on seeing this as a personal desertion? It's my job."

"You'll never understand. What if Danny hadn't gotten

better?'' she asked in desperation, trying to prove her point. "What if he was still sick? Would you go?"

"That's not fair! You're giving me a hypothetical situation."

She moved a good six inches away from him. "You're damn right! I want to know what will happen."

He looked as if he wanted to fold his arms around her and kiss away her anger. "You and Danny are important to me."

"Then don't go. Please, Nate. Don't go."

"Shara—"

"If you care about me and Danny, you won't go. You'll keep your promise and meet my mother."

"I can meet her another time. I can fly to England if I have to."

Shara shook her head. "You just don't see. You once accused me of running. You're running now. If you can't keep the small commitments, how are you ever going to keep big ones?"

"You're confusing the issue. You can't compare the importance of meeting your mother with photographing what might be the hurricane of the decade."

She looked at her son with sad eyes. "Something will *always* be more important than us. I never should have let you into my life. When I found out what you do, I should have cut it off."

He took her chin roughly in his hand. "Don't say that. Shara, we share something beautiful. You couldn't stop it from happening any more than I could."

"Yes, I could have. I should have. I can't handle this, Nate." Her voice wavered, then grew stronger as she steeled herself for what she had to say. "I can't handle your leaving at the sound of a phone call. I can't handle your being gone an indeterminate amount of time whenever it suits you. I don't want that uncertainty for Danny or for me."

He stroked her hair away from her cheek as if the tender touch could make her change her mind. "Don't make a decision now. This hurricane could fizzle out."

His gentleness was painful. It hurt instead of comforted because she knew she might have to live without it. "But there will be another one. Eventually. Or something else. I think . . . I think we should stop seeing each other. There's no point in torturing ourselves."

"Shara, don't end what's just beginning."

She couldn't look at him. She couldn't and keep the tears from spilling out. "I have no choice. The anger and betrayal I'm feeling would destroy anything we build. We'll grow farther and farther apart."

"I'm *not* Jim Nolan," Nate exploded, standing up. "I'll take care of you and Danny. I'll give you time and whatever else you want."

"When it's convenient for you," she said hopelessly, thinking not only of Jim but of her mother and stepfather.

"All right. What if I don't go?"

She shook her head dejectedly. "There's still the future. Other—"

"No," he interrupted. "What if I quit? What if I forget the job in Baltimore, forget taking this assignment? What if I spend my time running the newspaper and taking pictures as a hobby?"

A kernel of hope sprouted in her heart and she came to her feet. "Could you do that? Could you give it up?"

Indecision stamped his face and some other emotion, one that made him look as if he'd just given up his life. "I don't know. I have to do some serious thinking." His jaw flexed several times. "So do you. Because I don't think you can give me up any more than I can give you up. What we have is too strong."

He looked torn, lost, as worried about their future as she was. He took her in his arms and gave her a profound, unending kiss that reached beyond her senses, beyond her heart, right into her soul. She molded to him, kissed him back, seeking protection from the storm that could take him away from her.

But Nate tore his lips from hers and set her firmly away from him. His voice was raspy. "I'll come over tomorrow after work . . . after I've made a decision."

She felt dazed, afraid to be hopeful, afraid his decision would mean good-bye. "What if Halstein calls you?"

"I don't think he will since the system's stalled. If he does, I'll let you know." Nate kissed her forehead and headed for the door. He opened it and said, "Think about us, Shara. Long and hard."

She stared at the closed door, went to her son, picked him up, and hugged him—trying not to cry, trying to be the self-reliant mother she knew he needed.

Nate called Shara the next morning. Her hand shook when she heard his voice. "Did Halstein call you?"

"The system's still stalled. I'm going to wait until Danny's in bed to come over."

She couldn't tell anything from his tone. "You've made a decision?"

"We'll talk tonight."

"Why can't you tell me now?"

"Because we need to be face-to-face with no distractions."

"That doesn't sound good."

"Don't jump to conclusions. I'll see you around nine o'clock."

Shara put down the phone, filled with so many conflicting feelings. If Nate could choose a stable life, that would prove he loved her . . . and Danny. But would he regret what he was giving up? Would he blame her? Would he feel trapped? If he did, could they be happy? The other side of the coin . . . If he couldn't give it up?

She wouldn't compete again. Not with a career, not with a flirtation with excitement. She couldn't. What kind of life would that be for her? And what would happen to Danny when he became old enough to realize he couldn't count on his father?

That thought jolted Shara. She could see Nate as Danny's father. It was as simple as that, and as complex.

After Shara put Danny to bed, she felt cooped up and restless. She went outside to the patio. The evening shadows played over the concrete. Sitting on the metal glider, she pushed herself back and forth, trying to slow her heartbeat, trying to blank her mind. She closed her eyes, hoping she could shut out the fear.

The back door opened and shut. She opened her eyes. Nate's tie was askew. His hair was disheveled as if he had been running his fingers through it often. His eyes were deep gray and worried. She felt fear stronger than she had ever felt it before, fear that she would lose this man she loved.

He sat down next to her and ran his hand over the chair's arm. They glided for a few minutes, their rhythm smooth and unbroken. Shara finally said, "Tell me what you're going to do."

His long legs stilled their motion. "I want to be fair to both of us. I want us both to be sure of what we want."

"Nate, just tell me."

"I'm going to Hilton Head tomorrow morning." When he pleaded, "Shara, don't look at me like that," she knew he must be seeing the anguish in her heart.

She closed her eyes and took a deep breath. She felt him take her hands and say, "Listen to me." She opened her eyes again and waited. Waited for the explanation, the logic, the excuses.

"Shara, I have to go this time to find out if I can give it up. I have to be sure for both our sakes."

She felt strapped in place, paralyzed. "I don't understand."

"You were right when you said *I* had to make this decision." His eyes kept her immobile. "I have to make it freely. Remember when I went to Pittsburgh?"

"Yes," Shara answered, not comprehending where he was headed.

"We had had an argument. I was afraid I'd lose you." He settled her hands on his lap, pressed against his thigh. "I took some great pictures, but the whole thing wasn't as thrilling as it usually was. I thought I was preoccupied. But maybe assignments aren't important anymore. Maybe I can be happy sitting behind a desk. I have to take this assignment to find out."

She broke his hold and stared. "You have to go once more to see if you ever want to go again? This doesn't require a test trip, it requires a decision and maybe a commitment." Her voice had risen in intensity. Unable to contain her agitation, she rose from the glider and walked to the edge of the patio.

Nate followed her and clamped her shoulder to make her face him. "Don't you know I'm being torn up, too?" He gave her a level stare. "Neither of us has to go through this torture. If you could just accept . . ."

Tears spurted to her eyes. "I can't."

His voice was rough. "You won't."

"It's not a matter of will." She couldn't squelch the sob rising in her throat. "It's the loneliness and the pain of knowing I won't come first."

He looked totally exasperated, frustrated, close to angry. "Shara, a doctor has to think of his patients first. Can't you think of this the same way?"

He was looking for an out and she couldn't give it to him. Tears ran down her cheeks in twin streams. "No. Photographing a hurricane is not the same."

His expression was hard, so devoid of the gentleness she usually saw there. He wouldn't give in, she wouldn't give in. Neither of them could win. If Nate couldn't make a minor commitment and keep it, how could he keep something infinitely more serious? She couldn't live with him indefinitely without vows, without an indissolvable bond between them. Could Nate ever commit to marriage? The expression on his face said no. She couldn't stand to look at him and love him so deeply, knowing he'd never feel that way about her.

She turned away from him and ran into the house. When she reached the living room, he was two steps behind her. "Shara, we have to talk this through."

Her eyes blurred with tears. "It won't do any good."

He gave her a slight shake. "I *have* to do this. Trust me."

"Why should I?"

He went very quiet as his emotions poured from his eyes. "Because I love you."

He said it and felt no panic, no cage closing. Her tears were hot. When one fell on his arm, it burned with the extent of her pain. He couldn't bear to see her hurting, but he knew he had to go to Hilton Head. Just as he knew he had to show her as well as tell her exactly how much he loved her.

His lips swooped down and ambushed hers. He kissed her with tender but intense passion until she went limp against him. Swinging her into his arms, he carried her up the steps, not speaking, not asking her if she still wanted to run, not pausing on the landing.

Laying her on the bed, he kissed her again until the confusion in her eyes was replaced by passion. She reached for him and her fingers fumbled to undress him with the same desperation that made him clumsy. Their mouths sealed, their tongues mated, their hands reached, their legs intertwined. Only their love existed, only the here and now. There was no past or future. There was only the moment—precious, intense, excruciating because they knew it couldn't last.

Nate's fingers shook with the effort of restraining his need. But he was determined to love Shara in a way he had never loved her before, to brand her as his, to make her need their love and passion as much as she needed air to breathe.

As his sex, hard and determined, prodded the softness of Shara's thigh, Nate pulled his lips from hers. His voice was deep with emotion. "We're close, Shara. The love that binds us together can't be disputed, or denied, or put on a shelf because it isn't safe, or convenient. You need me as much as I need you. We belong together because we're right together, we fit together. We'll get through this, sweetheart, somehow, some way. Don't give up on us."

The tears in her eyes tinged her voice. "Don't go, Nate. Please. If you go . . ."

Nate kissed the tear on her cheek. "Shh. Don't think. Feel. Feel what we have."

Nate's mouth cherished her throat, told her her breasts were precious, revered her stomach, stoked the ferocity of her need.

He kissed the outline of the silky brown hair between her thighs. She opened her mouth to protest, but the words turned into a sigh of pleasure as he separated her legs. His tongue on her sensitive inner thighs made her whole body tremble. As Nate's lips and tongue loved her womanly essence, heat spread through her like a wave saturating a sandy beach. It receded, splashed forward, advancing farther than the time before. The sensation happened again and again until no part of her was left untouched. When the wave found the tips of her fingers, they curled around the bedspread to hold her steady, to keep her trembling from overwhelming her body.

"Nate. Nate, I love you," she gasped.

His heart felt as if it would burst with the rest of him. He felt the spasm shake her, felt the climax tighten her legs. He gave her a few moments to recover then aligned his body on top of hers. She was more than ready for him. When they fused, his lips met hers with all the loving fervor in his heart.

Nate's tongue and the matching motion of his body drove Shara to a new high. Her legs wrapped around his hips. Her hands locked behind his neck. She rocked with him until she felt like a sail blown by a furious wind to the end of the horizon and into another dimension. There were spirals and colors and earth, air, sea, and fire. She could see and feel and touch eternity.

Nate reached the same plane, his body shuddering again and again. Finally their bodies quieted. Nate shifted his weight to his side and gathered Shara tight in his arms.

THIRTEEN

When Shara awoke the next morning, she could hear the shower running. She and Nate had loved most of the night and when she slept, she had had a deep, dreamless sleep. She checked the clock. He was leaving in an hour. In that hour maybe she could convince him . . .

She untangled the sheets, snatched her robe from a hanger in the closet, and went downstairs to start breakfast. As she flipped French toast in the frying pan, she heard Nate come down the steps and go outside. A few minutes later he came back in and climbed the stairs. He must have kept his clothes in the van.

Fifteen minutes later, when she was arranging the toast on two plates, he appeared in the kitchen. She put their plates on the table.

Nate watched her carefully. He was dressed for traveling in a light-blue linen suit. The lines around his eyes and mouth were tight with the same tension that was making Shara's stomach clench.

He came to Shara and gathered her into his arms. "I could have had toast."

"You probably don't know when you'll eat next so I thought something hearty . . ." Her chin quivered and she knew she couldn't engage in inconsequential conversation. Laying her cheek against his shoulder, she held tight. "Change your mind, Nate. If you go to Hilton Head, you'll want to do this again and again. Prove that you love me. Stay here."

When Nate pulled back, anger thundered on his brow. "I *have* proven I love you . . . and Danny. Time and time again. It's the day-to-day living that counts, Shara. The hugs and kisses and talking and sharing. Why can't you see that?"

She shrugged away from him. "And why can't you see that your work will always come between us? If you go, Nate, I won't be waiting when you come home."

His arms went rigid at his sides. "What do you mean, you won't be waiting? I told you I'll make my decision—"

"You've *made* your decision. You're going. It will always be just this time . . . only one more time."

There was a mixture of anger and fear in his eyes. "Don't do this to us, Shara."

"*You're* the one who's doing it." Her voice became icy. "You'd better eat breakfast before it's too late." She sat down at the table.

Nate looked as if he wanted to shake her, but he clamped his lips together and sat down across from her. The silence was chilling as they poked at the French toast, both of them pretending to eat but only pushing the food around on their plates. The tension was as thick as molasses and the sadness couldn't be described.

Nate mechanically helped Shara put the breakfast items away. Finally he said, "I have to go."

She followed him to the foyer. When their eyes collided, she swallowed hard and said, "I'll pick up the things I have at your place while you're gone."

His cheeks flushed and the nerve in his jaw jumped. "Dammit, Shara! Don't make this decision now!"

"You've made yours. I've made mine."

He roughly pulled her into his arms and kissed her forcefully. Shara responded automatically. He changed the nature of the kiss until it became sweet, persuasively demanding. His tongue thrust into hers, swept her mouth, and asked for her surrender. She reacted as passionately as he did and Nate pulled her into his body so she could feel how much he needed her.

When Nate ended the kiss and pushed away, she knew he meant her to remember it along with their night of loving.

Picking up his suitcase and equipment bag, he said, "The hurricane should pass in a few days. They wreak havoc with communication systems—telephone and electric wires might be down. When I can get out safely, I'll drive to my mother's in Raleigh and call you from there."

"Don't call, Nate. A clean break will be best." She was playing her last card, gambling that her coolness would make him change his mind.

Obviously it didn't work. "You don't want a break any more than I do," he said.

The expression on his face when he saw the tears rolling down her cheeks made her want to dive into his arms. But she couldn't.

With a poignant look of tenderness, he said, "Remember, I love you." His eyes held hers. Then he opened the door.

Shara closed it. She heard the start of the van. She heard it back out of the driveway. She heard silence and she felt achingly alone.

Saturday evening, after a strained family meal, Chet told his wife he'd be back for her at eleven P.M. and left the townhouse to meet an old buddy. Shara's mother accepted his plans as if they were a common occurrence. She held Danny and played with him while Shara cleared the table.

After Shara stacked the dirty dishes in soapy water in the sink, she went to the living room. Pamela had Danny swinging in his swing and was watching a game show. She was as beautiful as ever. Her brown hair was perfectly coiffed, her makeup was impeccable, her designer blouse and skirt were without a crease. Only her wire-rimmed glasses seemed out of place. She'd only been wearing them the past two years.

Danny seemed to be fascinated by the colors and movement on the TV screen. Shara sat on the arm of the sofa and Pamela turned the TV off.

"Shara, is something wrong? You were almost . . . frozen with Chet tonight. Usually you try to be friendly."

A peacemaker. That's what her mother had always tried to be. "Maybe that's been a mistake. Maybe I should have told him a long time ago how I feel."

"It wouldn't do any good."

Shara looked at her mother with surprise. "I didn't think you ever tried!"

"I have. More lately. But he simply turns me off. He always has."

Shara didn't know what to say.

Pamela turned to face her daughter more squarely. "You feel sorry for me, don't you?"

"Mom . . ."

"You can tell me the truth."

Shara looked down at her lap. "You were a victim of circumstances. Chet gave you what you needed."

"And took away my self-respect. I let him take over my life for too long and now I can't get it back. When I found out you were pregnant, I realized I was going to be a grandmother and I didn't even know my own daughter."

"You did what you could."

"Which wasn't much. I'm surprised you don't hate me."

"I could never hate you, Mom. I . . . love you. You're my mother."

Pamela's eyes filled with tears. "Talk to me, honey. Tell me about your life."

"It might take more than an evening to do that."

"I know. I want more than one night with you and Danny." Her lips pursed and she nodded as if she'd come to a decision. "I'm going to stay in York while Chet visits his brother. That will give us until next Thursday. What do you say? Would you mind having me around?"

Shara was stunned. "Won't Chet get angry?"

"I don't care. I need to spend some time with you and Danny. And I think you need me here. Don't you?"

Tears welled up in Shara's eyes. "Maybe I do."

Her mother cleared her throat. "I couldn't help noticing a man's sneakers in the bathroom closet." She looked embarrassed. "I wasn't snooping. I needed a roll of toilet tissue."

Shara had forgotten to put the Nikes in the box with

the rest of Nate's belongings. She couldn't make herself go to his house. She'd thought of nothing but him since yesterday morning. Where was he? What was he doing? The hurricane was still stalled, picking up momentum. The experts were predicting it would hit land tomorrow afternoon.

"I was seeing someone."

"Was?" Shara's face must have shown reluctance to discuss the matter because Pamela said, "I'm sorry. I won't pry. We can talk about something else."

Shara missed Amber. Since she and Leon had married, they were rarely home. Shara needed to talk about Nate even if her mother couldn't help. She told her mother about Nate's career, about him delivering Danny, about his kindness, but also about his lust for adventure.

She ended with, "He's gone off to chase a hurricane and I told him I won't be waiting when he gets back."

Pamela let the silence emphasize Shara's words before she asked, "Do you want him to give up his career?"

Shara tossed her hair away from her face as she sat cross-legged on the floor next to Danny's swing. She felt drained, lost, alone. And angry. "He wouldn't be giving up his career. He'd have the newspaper. I want him to stop traveling and chasing thrills. He showed me today that's not possible."

"Shara, would you give up your career for him?"

"I'd put it on hold for Danny." She took Nate's key out of her shorts pocket and turned it over in her hand. She kept it with her to remind her of what she had to do.

"But would you give it up? Would you stop doing work that gave meaning to your life?"

"You can't compare my career and Nate's." Shara

didn't want to have to defend herself. She wanted some empathy.

But Pamela was intent on making her point. "Answer me, Shara. Would you give it up? Would you replace it with something that didn't give you as much satisfaction and happiness?"

Shara closed her hand around the key until it hurt. "It sounds as if you're on his side. I thought you wanted to know me better. To help me."

"Believe me, honey, helping doesn't always mean agreeing. I've learned that the hard way. I guess I'm trying to do for you what I could never do for myself. See reality for what it is. Why do you think you fell in love with Nate?"

Shara put the key back in her pocket, shifted her attention to her son, and wiggled each of Danny's toes, counting what she liked best about Nate. "Because he's strong, because he's honest, because he's—"

"Exciting?" her mother filled in.

Shara thought about that. He lived life to its fullest no matter what he did. Whether he was swimming, taking photographs, making love. "I guess he is."

"Was Jim exciting?" Pamela asked.

Shara's head snapped up and she was at a loss for words.

Her mother continued. "He fought fires. He saved lives. I think that's exciting."

Even though Shara herself had compared Nate and Jim, she knew they were *not* alike in the ways that mattered. "But Nate is steady and dependable, too. He knows how to take responsibility for what he does. I trust him with Danny as much as I trust myself. I don't think I could have trusted Jim. I would have been afraid he wasn't giving him undivided attention because he'd have one ear on the monitor and he might let him fall or hurt himself. Nate's so careful, so dependable.''

Pamela took off her glasses and pointed the sidepiece at Shara. "It seems to me what you want Nate to give up is part of why you were attracted to him.''

"I didn't know he still did this." Shara rubbed her hands along her calves. "So how could I have been attracted to him because of it?''

"Honey, it's part of Nate's makeup. You take it away and he won't be the same man.''

"That's nonsense!''

Her mother didn't rise to her daughter's outraged tone. "No, it's not. You think about it. You're asking Nate to give up some of himself, a part of him you love. Aren't you?''

Shara returned to an old argument—one that played in her head like a well-worn record. "If he loved me enough, he'd want to stay with me and Danny.''

Pamela sat forward on the couch. "Shara, isn't it better to have his caring and his love and his undivided attention when he's home than not to have it at all? Chet doesn't travel. We spend time together doing activities. But he rarely really listens to me. I rarely have his presence. If Nate is the man you've described, I'd say you're a lucky woman and he's a man worth loving. Maybe he needs to know you won't smother him before he can make a commitment.''

Shara felt as if the wind had been knocked from her sails. Could her mother be right? Did she love Nate *because* he was exciting? If she could close him in a box, did she love him the way she should? Unconditionally? She was confused and she had to sort it all out.

As if she was holding up a mirror, Pamela insisted Shara look at the reflection of the past. "Aren't you afraid that if Nate pursues this career, you'll end up on the sidelines like you did with Jim?"

Pamela had visited her and Jim twice a year. "I never realized you'd perceived so much."

"I might not have done well with my own life, but that doesn't mean I can't see what's happening with yours."

Shara dropped her eyes, avoiding what her mother was attempting to make her see. "Mom, I don't want to be convenient, or nice to have around, or an appendage. I want to be a vital part of Nate's life."

"Think about Nate. Think about all the time you've known him," Pamela prompted. "Does he respect you? Does he consider your opinion? Does he ever put you down?"

Shara remembered the first day she met Nate. It seemed like years ago. She had walked into his office, telling him the strategies of stress management. Their eyes had connected much more often than they should have. She remembered him looking down at her hand and seeing her wedding ring. There had been a change in his attitude and he'd put distance between them. Until he held her when Jim died. Some of the distance vanished and in the months that followed, he'd become a friend. The day Danny was born, there was no more distance. They bonded. That bond had grown into something real and good and glorious.

He did respect her. He affirmed her. He made her feel feminine and special. Shara brought her eyes to her mother's. "I *am* afraid his job will pull him away from me."

"It won't if you trust each other. If you love each other

enough. I've never had a relationship like that, Shara. But maybe you can."

Shara had a lot of thinking to do. Thinking that had to be finished before Nate returned.

The barometer was falling tenth by tenth as Nate walked the beach at Hilton Head. The sunrise had been a brilliant red. The TV crew was waiting for him farther up the beach. They had to evacuate. Shelters had been set up about fifty miles inland—church social rooms, school cafeterias, fire halls.

The level of the ocean was rising slowly. Long swells hit the shore in a slow rhythm different from the usual waves. In a few hours the ocean would rise in hurricane tides. High cirrus clouds spread across the sky, converging at the center of the horizon.

Nate shot picture after picture, wishing Shara was with him so she could witness the unnatural beauty. When the system stalled again after he had arrived, he almost called her. But he'd decided against it. She didn't want to hear from him. He gave a vicious oath and stuffed his hands in his jeans pockets while he looked at the horizon. Maybe if she saw the pictures he'd left in the darkroom, she'd realize what they had together. All he could do now was ride this thing out. And hope. Hope like hell he hadn't destroyed their chance at a future.

Nate turned when he heard a sharp whistle. The head of the news crew was beckoning to him. He took off at a run.

Shara watched the Sunday-morning news. The weatherman was predicting the hurricane would hit the shores of South Carolina in four to six hours. She wondered if Nate was safe in a shelter, or if he was on a beach waiting for the monster. She chewed on her lower lip. She wanted to feel close to him. She wished there was some way she could make contact. Suddenly she knew she could. In his house. She'd feel closer to him there than anywhere else.

She picked Danny up from the blanket she had laid on the floor. "Come on, buster. We're going to visit Nate's house. If you cooperate, I might even show you his darkroom."

Shara made good her word. While Danny bobbed in the baby carrier around her neck, she walked through Nate's house, her decision to cut off their relationship abruptly forgotten. His office looked as if he was still working. Papers were strewn across the desk. His brown moccasins lay under the chair. She went into the bedroom. A shirt was thrown across the bedroom chair. She picked it up, folded it against her nose, and sniffed. It smelled like him. His scent made him real, safe, in the room with her. She remembered their last night of loving and tears came to her eyes.

She loved him. The longing to have his arms around her was a tangible ache. She put the shirt down. She had thought about her stepfather and Jim and Nate in the past twenty-four hours. She hadn't thought about much else. The three men were now separate in her mind, not linked together. Jim and Chet represented the past, Nate the future.

She went downstairs through the kitchen and down to the basement. Opening the door to the darkroom, she switched on the light. Contact sheets were clothespinned on the drying line, and she wondered if Nate had let them hang on purpose.

There were poses of Danny in his portable crib on the

terrace, in his car seat, on a blanket. There were shots of her with Danny, by herself. And then there was a third sheet of all three of them that Nate had taken on time delay. He had circled one shot with a grease pencil. Danny was missing. She and Nate were standing by a tree facing each other. They were close enough to kiss and passion gleamed in their eyes.

A feeling of belonging squeezed her so hard, she leaned back against the work table. Nate's pictures told the truth. He would be a wonderful husband and a wonderful father no matter what he did for a living. Her mother had been right. He *was* a man worth loving. He'd love her and Danny with all he was capable of giving. With Nate, that would be more love than she could ever experience with anyone. She was sure of that now, as sure as she was of her love for Danny.

But now that she was sure, what did Nate feel? She had given him an ultimatum. That could have destroyed his love for her. She had asked him not to push her, but she had pushed him, and pushed some more. If she told him she'd accept his career, would he believe her? Or would he always remember that last scene when she told him she wouldn't wait? Would he think that would happen again?

She had been foolish to think she could give up his love . . . ever. Each day they'd have together she would cherish. They would have love and life and pictures full of memories.

She had to tell him that. But she couldn't get to him. The hurricane would make it impossible. She'd have to wait. And hope. And put a speech together that would convince him her love didn't come with a price tag.

FOURTEEN

The cafeteria buzzed with voices trying to drown out the mighty storm outside as Nate searched for a vantage point. He and the TV crew had driven through sporadic showers that were fast becoming a pounding rain. Walking around the shelter, he poked into nooks and crannies.

In the kitchen, a compact clothes dryer was stacked on top of the washing machine. It was vented outside. Nate took off the outside apparatus. When he returned to the inside, he maneuvered the camera until the lens slid into the hole. He packed cardboard around it to hold it steady.

A youngster sidled up beside him. "Watcha doin', mister?"

Nate grinned. "I'm going to take pictures of the hurricane."

"You can't. You'll get wet."

A ten-year-old was practical. Nate looked at the boy's curly brown hair. Would Danny's wave like that when he was older? "I won't get wet because the camera's here, on the inside. See?"

208

The boy looked at it carefully. "Can I help?"

"What's your name?"

"Rodney."

"Well, Rodney, I won't need much help. But when the hurricane really hits, you can snap a few pictures for me. In the meantime, I have another camera over at the table. Do you want to see how it works?"

His brown eyes grew wide. "Sure!"

In the next few hours, Nate made friends with Rodney, met his parents, helped board up the windows, and socialized with people native to the area who were worried about their houses and belongings. The downpour changed into a raging force. Winds increased and wailed with ferocity. Water beat, poured, smashed.

While the brunt of the hurricane hit, Nate snapped two rolls of film, let Rodney snap a few, then took the camera out and boarded the aperture from inside. The wind howled, the building shook, objects crashed against the building, some of them hitting each other. The winds screeched, gusting higher and higher. The force was a creature tearing the small town apart.

All of a sudden, Nate realized conversation had ceased. An old gent sitting in a lawn chair said, "The eye's passin' over. Listen."

The wind had stopped. So had the beating rain. Nate knew he had to make his move. He called to a member of the TV crew, "Jeff, I'm going out."

The veteran reporter called back, "Ten minutes, Nate. No more. You get your butt back in here."

Nate gave an okay sign with his thumb and forefinger, picked up his camera, and hurried to the door.

Once outside, he stood in awe. From what he had read, he realized a cloud wall surrounded the hurricane's eye, and he knew the eye was deceiving. The weather seemed serene. The sun was even shining. But it was an eerie peace and he knew the other half of the hurricane was coming. The wind would blow in the opposite direction.

He started snapping pictures of broken tree trunks, tangled power lines, shingles blown off a house roof. He got caught up in destruction surrounded by calm, caught up in the challenge of being somewhere few others would dare to be. Walking across water-sodden grass, he snapped the flooding water in the gutters and took pictures from every possible direction.

In the blink of a shutter, conditions changed. The sky grew black, the wind began as a breeze but headed toward vehemence. Nate realized he'd pushed his luck and stayed out too long. When he turned toward the building, his heart jumped to his throat. Rodney was standing outside, watching him! Wasn't someone supervising the boy? Hadn't anyone missed him? In God's name, why had he come outside? Nate waved his arm, trying to motion the boy inside. But Rodney waved back.

Nate heard the boy yell, "I want to help you."

"Go in. Go in *now*," Nate shouted as he started running, faster than he'd ever run.

The gale screeched. Out of nowhere a roof shingle hurled past Nate and he understood the jeopardy he was in. The jeopardy he'd put Rodney in. If he hadn't insisted on photographing the eye . . . As he ran toward the boy, Nate pictured an older Danny instead. What would happen if he pulled this kind of stunt when Nate wasn't around? What if a baby-sitter looked away for a few minutes? What if . . . ?

Nate's legs couldn't pump vigorously enough. With insight born from the chance he could lose his life or be torn apart by the winds of nature, he knew he was running away from the thirst of adventure and toward a life with Shara. No exclusive photograph, no sensational story was worth losing his life or the woman and child he loved.

Rodney seemed paralyzed by the vicious nature swirling around him. He was literally scared stiff. A flying branch hit Nate's shoulder and stung his face as the rain drove against him making Rodney and the cafeteria seem farther than they were. The forces of earth whirled around him in confusion, paying no mind to a man stupid enough to find himself caught in the vengeance of a hurricane or a boy foolish enough to follow him.

Five more yards. Jeff appeared at the door to the cafeteria. Out of the corner of Nate's eye he saw a hefty portion of a narrow tree sailing toward Rodney. Nate lunged toward the boy and protected him with his own body. A second later, he felt a crashing thud and murky blackness overtook him.

Pamela folded Danny's diapers and stacked them under the dressing table. "Chet called me last night."

Shara pulled up Danny's rubber pants then fitted his chubby legs into red shorts. "Was he still angry?"

"Amazingly, no. He said you don't have to drive me to the airport to meet him. He'll pick me up and we'll go together."

"Is the wind direction changing?"

"I doubt it. We're both set in our ways. Thing is, he's ten years older than me and wants my company when he retires. In a crazy way, we need each other. But it's nice to know I have a little clout." Pamela straightened the bottle of baby lotion and jar of Vaseline. "Speaking of wind, have you heard any more reports on the hurricane clean-up?''

''Communication is being restored. Thirty feet of beach at Hilton Head was eroded by the waves. It's a good thing the hurricane blew inland and lost most of its oomph. The downed power lines and flooding are still making travel difficult. I just wish I knew where Nate was.''

The doorbell rang. ''I'll get it,'' Pamela said. ''You finish dressing Danny.''

Shara urged Danny's arms into a navy-blue tank top. They were going to take him for a walk and the temperature was in the nineties again. At least now the air-conditioning worked.

She lifted Danny to her shoulder, bouncing him slightly and humming to him. But when she reached the bottom of the stairs, her throat clogged. Nate was standing in the foyer talking to her mother.

''I was just telling Nate that we kept track of the storm,'' Pamela said. ''It looks like he got caught in the middle of it.''

Shara's eyes went to his face. A gauze strip went from his cheekbone to his jawline with heavy bruising outlining it. He was pale and there were circles under his eyes. Something had happened. Somehow Nate had gotten hurt. She wanted to kiss him, hold him, make love to him. Doubts pommeled her. Maybe he'd come to pick up his clothes. Maybe he was going to tell her they were finished because he couldn't choose her above his career. Maybe he had been preoccupied by their argument and that's why he'd gotten hurt.

''What happened?'' she asked in a voice that sounded more like a croak.

Pamela took charge and plucked Danny out of her

daughter's arms. "You two can't stand here and talk. Go get comfortable in the living room. I'll take Danny for that walk. The stroller's on the patio so I'll leave by the back door."

All at once, Shara had no more doubts. She loved Nate and she was going to convince him of that. Nothing mattered except being with him. He was here. She would love him forever. She wanted to bury herself in his arms. But she couldn't yet. His eyes were unreadable.

"What's under the bandage?" she asked quietly.

"A few scratches." At her glare, he amended, "Okay. One very big scratch."

Shara noticed his hair was ruffled on the left side of his head. She couldn't stop her hand from reaching up and touching it. There was a large lump. "Nate." She backed up.

"Don't say anything until I tell you what I've come up with."

"Nate, I want to tell you—"

"Shara, you were right. I was running. I'm sorry I broke my promise to you. I'm going to make some changes in my life and I want you to be part of them—"

"I don't want to force you to make a decision. I was wrong. I didn't mean to emotionally blackmail you—"

"When a tree trunk almost hit a little boy because of me, I realized you and Danny will always come first—"

"I'll stand by you no matter what you do—"

Shara stopped. "A tree trunk?"

"You'll stand by me?" Nate repeated.

Shara gave him a crooked smile. "We're not listening to each other and everything's getting confused. Can I please go first so I can get this out?"

"Only if you promise me I can try and change your

mind if it's not what I want to hear." When she nodded, Nate crossed his arms over his chest like a shield. He resembled a gladiator about to do battle.

Shara almost smiled, but knew they had to be serious first. "I had to work through some things—the reasons why my marriage failed, the reasons I felt betrayed by my stepfather and Jim, why I wanted to keep you in York. I was afraid your career would take you away from me— not in miles, but in emotional distance. I guess I didn't believe I was lovable enough to keep your interest."

He uncrossed his arms. "Sweetheart, you're the most lovable person I know."

Her smile was radiant as she relished the pleasure of just looking at him. "I guess I've decided I'm worth loving and you're worth loving. Without conditions. Mom helped me see that your career has made you the man you are today. I love that man, so I can't hate his career. If you want to keep chasing hurricanes, I can't say I'll ever understand it, but I can accept it. If you're not doing what makes you happy, you'll be a different person. I love you the way you are."

Nate closed the distance between them and enfolded her in his arms. A few moments later, he stepped back and said huskily, "You've just given me the most beautiful gift I've ever received—your love and your trust. Do you know how much I love you?"

"I'm beginning to," she murmured, her eyes still on his. "Nate, I'm sorry I put us through this."

He kissed the apology from her lips, took her hand, and pulled her to the sofa in the living room. "I have a few things to tell you."

A lump lodged in her throat. "About how you got hurt?"

"Yes." He cuddled her against his shoulder. "A few moments are going to change our lives. I got the beauty and fake stillness of the eye of the hurricane on film. But I took too long. Gusts suddenly started up, rain in sheets. I'd made friends with a little boy in the shelter. He followed me outside without anyone knowing. Because of me, he almost got killed. What if he'd been Danny? What would happen if I took off and you and Danny needed me? I'd never forgive myself. And you wouldn't forgive me, either. A member of the news team pulled us both to safety. When I came to, you were all I thought about. I realized what you had been trying to tell me."

She gently touched the gauze patch and the bruising around it. "Are you sure you're all right? Shouldn't you be in a hospital?"

"A doctor checked me out. I have a headache and a bump but no other symptoms. I wanted to fly home yesterday, but he made me promise to wait until he checked me again this morning. I feel a little battered, but I'm fine."

"Thank God."

His arm pressed her closer. "I'm going to quit globetrotting. I'm staying here with you and Danny."

"But you love what you do."

"I love you and Danny more."

She doused the desire she always felt in his arms to resolve an important question. "Won't you feel trapped? Can you stand to just sit behind a desk?"

"I won't feel trapped because I'm making a free choice. I can be happy running the paper." His eyes twinkled mysteriously, matching his secretive smile. "But I've thought of a couple of projects that might solve my field fever and your problems, too."

"My problems?" she asked, thinking all her problems were over.

"You want to stay home with Danny, but you like your work. How would you like to work on a book with me?"

Excitement fluttered. Working with Nate could be fun, challenging. "What kind of book?"

"You gave me the idea. You said I'm good at capturing faces." He smoothed down her blouse collar, letting his fingers linger at the point of the V. "Why don't we do a book about children for health-care professionals to give to their patients? I'll do the photographs, you do the nutritional and emotional information so parents can learn how to keep their kids healthy. What do you think?"

His finger was rough against her skin and she longed to feel his hand on her breast. With difficulty, she kept her mind on the conversation. "Is there a market?"

Nate watched the rise and fall of the pocket on her blouse. "There is. When I called Halstein and told him I got his hurricane but I wouldn't be taking his job, I asked for his opinion. He said he'd be interested in publishing it himself. He's a mercenary at heart and he grabs anything he thinks might be successful. He also suggested I put together a coffee-table book of disaster pictures." Nate lifted his hand to Shara's chin and stroked it with his thumb. "Will you do this with me?"

"It's what you *really* want to do?"

His eyes seemed to swallow her. "Along with marrying you and being Danny's father."

She licked her lower lip and heard his heart thump louder. "Marry me?"

"Yep. Will you?"

"Oh, Nate." She brushed a tear from her cheek. "Yes, I'll marry you."

His kiss was long and hard and passionate. But something was niggling at her mind. Something she had to ask. She held his face between her hands and pulled back. "You won't get bored?"

His grin was devilish and thoroughly sexy. "With you and Danny around? That's not likely."

She tried to clear her head of X-rated thoughts until they settled this. "You have to promise me something."

"Anything."

"If you do get bored, if you get restless, you'll go back into the field."

"If I get restless, I'll get back into the field but in a different way. How would you like to take a mule ride down the Grand Canyon? Danny can go along in a backpack."

He was always taking her by surprise. She guessed she'd have to get used to that. "Are you serious?"

"Sure. We could do a series on adventures for families." His hand began moving possessively over her hip. "We could travel together. Maybe I'll think of buying a magazine or starting one myself. Sweetheart, the possibilities are endless as long as I have you and Danny with me."

"We'll be with you. Always," she vowed with every ounce of her love.

He slid his arm under her knees and scooped her onto his lap. "I was surprised to find your mother here."

Shara toyed with the buttons on his knit shirt. "She's been a big help."

As she caressed his uninjured cheek, he said, "You can tell me all about it later. Your mother's the last thing on my mind at this moment."

Shara's head bobbed up and she grinned impishly.

"What *is* on your mind? The weather? The price of tea in China . . . ?"

He pinched her behind. "Sassy, aren't you?"

She thumped his chest with her palm. "As sassy as you are . . . Now what's that word? Lascivious."

"Lascivious? You come here." He tilted his knees up so she fell against his chest. His lips caressed hers and his tongue repetitively stroked hers as his hand moved up and down her spine.

When he brought his head up, there was an ocean of love in his eyes washing over her. His strong arms tightened in shelter around her. "Loving you has brought meaning to my life. Instead of imprisoning me, it's given me freedom."

Shara lifted her lips for another kiss—a kiss that would assure him that would never change.

EPILOGUE

Shara hesitated outside the door of Nate's office. She should probably do this differently—with candlelight, a sexy negligee. Not that she needed one around Nate. A year hadn't dimmed his love or his passion. But now . . .

The door was ajar and she pushed it open. "Hi. Are you busy?"

Nate rolled his chair away from his desk and gave her a look that always wobbled her knees. "Never too busy for you. I have something to show you."

She closed the door behind her and raised her brows suggestively. "Here? Mr. McKendrick!"

"Come here, woman," he demanded as he shuffled papers on his desk to find what he was looking for. "Hot off the presses. Halstein sent a box this morning."

Shara took the booklet from him and stared proudly at the cover. Her name and Nate's appeared under the face of their child. Tears came to her eyes as she turned the pages. "It's wonderful, isn't it?"

"I think we're prejudiced. Give me a kiss, then we'll discuss it."

His voice slid over her like hot honey, and when he stood and pulled her into his arms, she melted against him. The kiss contained as much wonder and discovery as the first time. When he came up for air, she pushed against his chest with the heels of her hands. "I have something to tell you."

"Uh oh. Good or bad?"

She hoped the twinkle wouldn't leave his eyes. "I think it's very good, but I don't know what you'll think."

"Well?"

She took a breath. "Uh, you know, we haven't been very careful the last few months when we've made love. I mean, I didn't always have the chance to put in the diaphragm and . . . uh . . . I just saw the doctor and . . . I'm pregnant."

For a moment Nate stood perfectly still. Then, after a loud whoop, he swung her around in a circle. "That's the best news I've heard since you said you'd marry me."

Breathless, and a little dizzy, she admitted, "But somehow I got the idea you might not want more children."

He hugged her. "That's changed since we've been married. I love being with Danny. And I wanted another child . . . our child. Why do you think we made love by the stream, and on the swing, and . . ."

"You planned this?"

He looked boyishly naughty. "Not exactly. But I'm damned pleased with the result. Why didn't you tell me you suspected you were pregnant?"

"I thought our trip to San Francisco threw my body off and I wanted to make sure before I told you."

Nate's fingers went to the buttons on her blouse while

his eyes meaningfully looked toward the leather couch. "Now, you've told me and I think we should celebrate."

"Nate! What if Jerry . . . ?"

Nate left her for a moment to lock the door. "Jerry knows better. Since the last time he caught us kissing in here, he doesn't barge in. If the door's locked, he'll come back later."

Nate had added so much fun to her life, spontaneity, love. Her fingers went to his tie and nudged the knot open. "If we celebrate now, does that mean we can't celebrate tonight?"

"Sweetheart, we can celebrate until the doctor tells us to stop. And even then, I'm *sure* we can be creative."

She twined her arms around his neck. "Do you know how much I love you?"

"Yep. But I'm not adverse to having you show me."

With alacrity, she did.

SHARE THE FUN . . .
SHARE YOUR NEW-FOUND TREASURE!!

You don't want to let your new books out of your sight? That's okay. Your friends can get their own. Order below.

No. 25 LOVE WITH INTEREST by Darcy Rice
Stephanie & Elliot find $47,000,000 *plus* interest—true love!

No. 26 NEVER A BRIDE by Leanne Banks
The last thing Cassie wanted was a relationship. Joshua had other ideas.

No. 27 GOLDILOCKS by Judy Christenberry
David and Susan join forces and get tangled in their own web.

No. 28 SEASON OF THE HEART by Ann Hammond
Can Lane and Maggie's newfound feelings stand the test of time?

No. 29 FOSTER LOVE by Janis Reams Hudson
Morgan comes home to claim his children but Sarah claims his heart.

No. 30 REMEMBER THE NIGHT by Sally Falcon
Joanna throws caution to the wind. Is Nathan fantasy or reality?

No. 31 WINGS OF LOVE by Linda Windsor
Mac & Kelly soar to new heights of ecstasy. Are they ready?

No. 32 SWEET LAND OF LIBERTY by Ellen Kelly
Brock has a secret and Liberty's freedom could be in serious jeopardy!

No. 33 A TOUCH OF LOVE by Patricia Hagan
Kelly seeks peace and quiet and finds paradise in Mike's arms.

No. 34 NO EASY TASK by Chloe Summers
Hunter is wary when Doone delivers a package that will change his life.

No. 35 DIAMOND ON ICE by Lacey Dancer
Diana could melt even the coldest of hearts. Jason hasn't a chance.

No. 36 DADDY'S GIRL by Janice Kaiser
Slade wants more than Andrea is willing to give. Who wins?

No. 37 ROSES by Caitlin Randall
It's an inside job & K.C. helps Brett find more than the thief!

No. 38 HEARTS COLLIDE by Ann Patrick
Matthew finds big trouble and it's spelled P-a-u-l-a.

No. 39 QUINN'S INHERITANCE by Judi Lind
Gabe and Quinn share an inheritance and find an even greater fortune.

No. 40 CATCH A RISING STAR by Laura Phillips
Justin is seeking fame; Beth helps him find something more important.

No. 41 SPIDER'S WEB by Allie Jordan
Silvia's quiet life explodes when Fletcher shows up on her doorstep.

No. 42 TRUE COLORS by Dixie DuBois
Julian helps Nikki find herself again but will she have room for him?

No. 43 DUET by Patricia Collinge
Adam & Marina fit together like two perfect parts of a puzzle!

No. 44 DEADLY COINCIDENCE by Denise Richards
J.D.'s instincts tell him he's not wrong; Laurie's heart says trust him.

No. 45 PERSONAL BEST by Margaret Watson
Nick is a cynic; Tess, an optimist. Where does love fit in?

No. 46 ONE ON ONE by JoAnn Barbour
Vincent's no saint but Loie's attracted to the devil in him anyway.

No. 47 STERLING'S REASONS by Joey Light
Joe is running from his conscience; Sterling helps him find peace.

No. 48 SNOW SOUNDS by Heather Williams
In the quiet of the mountain, Tanner and Melaine find each other again.

Meteor Publishing Corporation
Dept. 192, P. O. Box 41820, Philadelphia, PA 19101-9828

Please send the books I've indicated below. Check or money order only—no cash, stamps or C.O.D.s (PA residents, add 6% sales tax). I am enclosing $2.95 plus 75¢ handling fee for *each* book ordered.

Total Amount Enclosed: $_____.

___ No. 25	___ No. 31	___ No. 37	___ No. 43
___ No. 26	___ No. 32	___ No. 38	___ No. 44
___ No. 27	___ No. 33	___ No. 39	___ No. 45
___ No. 28	___ No. 34	___ No. 40	___ No. 46
___ No. 29	___ No. 35	___ No. 41	___ No. 47
___ No. 30	___ No. 36	___ No. 42	___ No. 48

Please Print:
Name _____

Address _____ Apt. No. _____

City/State _____ Zip _____

Allow four to six weeks for delivery. Quantities limited.